Lang's warning yell brought Bolan around in a tight crouch

He saw Lang, one hand thrown out to warn Bolan back, his other bringing his own weapon into play. The DEA agent was between Bolan and a line of armed hardmen.

"Resist, and you will die right now, Belasko! There is no way you can win."

There were too many of them, their weapons up and gleaming dully. Bolan allowed the Uzi to slip from his hand.

"Sensible," the lead gunner said, moving toward the agent. "I hope Lang sees the situation in the same way."

Lang began to lower his weapon, until the advancing figure reached him. Then he gave a wild yell and yanked the Uzi back on line.

The dark figure barely paused. He raised the pistol he'd been concealing at his side. There was a single shot, a powerful, heavy sound as the weapon roared, the muzzle no more than three feet from Lang's head. The slug cored his skull and erupted from the other end in a dark spray. Lang was thrown to the ground, his body going into spasms.

The killer pulled his weapon around, leveling it at Bolan, his finger against the trigger. He moved forward, turning slightly so the light played across his face.

"You want the same way out, Belasko?" Gabriel Lorenz asked, smiling.

MACK BOLAN ®

The Executioner

DON PENDLETON'S
EXECUTIONER®
THE
END GAME

END GAME

All rights reserved. Except for use in any review, the reproduction or utilization of this work in whole or in part in any form by any electronic, mechanical or other means, now known or hereafter invented, including xerography, photocopying and recording, or in any information storage or retrieval system, is forbidden without the permission of the publisher, Worldwide Library, 225 Duncan Mill Road, Don Mills, Ontario, Canada M3B 3K9.

All characters in this book have no existence outside the imagination of the author and have no relation whatsoever to anyone bearing the same name or names. They are not even distantly inspired by any individual known or unknown to the author, and all incidents are pure invention.

® are Trademarks registered in the United States Patent and Trademark Office and in other countries.

A GOLD EAGLE BOOK FROM
WORLDWIDE®

TORONTO • NEW YORK • LONDON
AMSTERDAM • PARIS • SYDNEY • HAMBURG
STOCKHOLM • ATHENS • TOKYO • MILAN
MADRID • WARSAW • BUDAPEST • AUCKLAND

First edition February 1997
ISBN 0-373-64218-0

Special thanks and acknowledgment to
Mike Linaker for his contribution to this work.

END GAME

To try to win a war, to set victory as an aim, is pure madness, since total war with nuclear weapons will be fatal to both sides.

—B. H. Liddell Hart, *Defense or Deterence*, 1962

We have made nuclear weapons a valuable commodity, something to be traded for wealth and power. We must not forget that they are instruments of war. We cannot allow them to get into the wrong hands. The cost to life is too high.

—Mack Bolan

THE
MACK BOLAN®
LEGEND

Nothing less than a war could have fashioned the destiny of the man called Mack Bolan. Bolan earned the Executioner title in the jungle hell of Vietnam.

But this soldier also wore another name—Sergeant Mercy. He was so tagged because of the compassion he showed to wounded comrades-in-arms and Vietnamese civilians.

Mack Bolan's second tour of duty ended prematurely when he was given emergency leave to return home and bury his family, victims of the Mob. Then he declared a one-man war against the Mafia.

He confronted the Families head-on from coast to coast, and soon a hope of victory began to appear. But Bolan had broken society's every rule. That same society started gunning for this elusive warrior—to no avail.

So Bolan was offered amnesty to work within the system against terrorism. This time, as an employee of Uncle Sam, Bolan became Colonel John Phoenix. With a command center at Stony Man Farm in Virginia, he and his new allies—Able Team and Phoenix Force—waged relentless war on a new adversary: the KGB.

But when his one true love, April Rose, died at the hands of the Soviet terror machine, Bolan severed all ties with Establishment authority.

Now, after a lengthy lone-wolf struggle and much soul-searching, the Executioner has agreed to enter an "arm's-length" alliance with his government once more, reserving the right to pursue personal missions in his Everlasting War.

1

Northeast Scotland

Rain lashed the windshield of Bolan's car as he sat in a parking lot across from a hotel in a small Scottish town.

Intelligence from Stony Man Farm had brought him to this windswept spot on the northeastern coast of Scotland, where he now waited to spot two men, one of them a professional assassin.

The Executioner wondered why a man like Ray Kasden had been hired to come to a place like this. That Kasden was a gun for hire was certain, but why was he in the Scottish boonies?

Bolan glanced at his watch. He'd been waiting more than two hours. He'd arrived in Scotland early the previous afternoon. A car had been waiting for him at Aberdeen airport, and he'd driven up the coast until he reached the small hotel where a room had been booked for him. According to the information provided by the Farm, his final destination lay a few miles farther north, easily reached by a thirty-minute drive.

In his hotel room, he'd checked out the small executive case that had been stowed away in the trunk of the car. Inside was a Beretta 93-R pistol, a number of additional clips of 9 mm ammunition, and a shoulder rig for the weapon.

As the rain continued to pelt his car, Bolan mentally reviewed the lead-in to his latest mission.

Hyatt Regency Hotel, Washington

MACK BOLAN WALKED across the lobby of the hotel. Spotting Hal Brognola's broad figure, he cut through the crowd toward the man.

"Glad you could make it," Brognola said.

"Am I using my Mike Belasko cover?" the Executioner asked.

The big Fed nodded. "The guy we're meeting is Dr. Marcus Kaminski. He's a physicist at the Arms Control Association here in Washington. As we discussed, you're a writer doing an article about terrorists building nuclear devices. I think you'll pick up what it's all about pretty fast."

Bolan took that as a wait-and-see.

"You'd better use this," Brognola said, handing him a reporter's notebook.

The big Fed led the way to the lounge and the table where Kaminski was waiting.

The doctor in no way represented the stereotypical scientist. Standing, he was close to Bolan's own height and had the shoulders of a linebacker. His grip when he shook Bolan's hand was strong.

When they were seated, Brognola addressed Bolan.

"I asked for this meeting with Dr. Kaminski because I don't have the knowledge to give you the kind of information you need," Brognola said. "I explained what you're after for your article."

"I'm a good listener, Doctor," Bolan prompted.

Kaminski spoke quietly, yet clearly, detailing for Bolan why Brognola's summons had been so hasty and urgent.

"Uranium 235, which you've probably heard of, is one of the materials that can be used for the core of a nuclear device. Plutonium is the more favored element, but it requires a highly sophisticated triggering mechanism. To create the nuclear explosion, plutonium has to be set off by precisely timed explosions that crush it into a critical mass. This kind of device is very difficult to manufacture, and everything has to be made to precise limits.

"A uranium-235 bomb, however, doesn't need such intricate mechanisms. To detonate a uranium core, all you need to do is fire another piece of uranium into it with enough force, and this will trigger the chain reaction.

"The comparative simplicity of this means that anyone who can get hold of the raw materials, and have them correctly formed, has the components for a small, but effective nuclear device. It's small by military standards, but it'll contain enough power to destroy a few city blocks and dump enough radioactive fallout to kill thousands of people later on."

Bolan knew this already, but he scribbled down the salient points to maintain his cover. At the same time he figured that Brognola didn't want him to have this information so he could conduct a seminar on the construction of a nuclear device. The big Fed was going to give him the bad news later, and Bolan had an idea what that would be.

He turned his attention back to Kaminski.

"You don't find nuclear bomb builders on many street corners," he said.

Kaminski smiled. "True," he agreed. "But there are people around who could do it, for a price. If someone's got the materials, then we can assume they've also got somebody who can put it together."

"You're not making my day, Doctor," Bolan said.

"Mr. Brognola knew that when he asked me to speak to you. I admit that what I'm describing isn't going to help me sleep easier at night, either."

"I wanted Mr. Belasko to have firsthand information for his article," Brognola stated. "We want factual writing, not scaremongering nonsense."

"I understand," Kaminski replied. He handed Bolan a manila envelope. "There's some additional information in there. It really just expands on what I've explained, but it might give you some guidance. My home office telephone numbers are included if you need to contact me."

Kaminski glanced at his watch and stood.

"Thank you for your time, Doctor," Brognola said.

"Mr. Belasko, I hope I've been of help."

"Does he have anything more to do with this?" Bolan asked after the doctor had left.

Brognola leaned back in his chair.

"This goes back a few months. As you know, the Organized Crime Department, or OCD, is part of the Russian police service. Our own people have been working with them where interests overlap. Mainly we've been giving the Russians guidance on how to combat organized crime, but occasionally other information is traded. A source confirmed that thefts of uranium 235 have been occurring over a period of time. The Russians suspected this for a while, but they couldn't get anything definite on it until a guy called Grushev was found shot to pieces. Before he died, he did some talking, enough to arouse the interests of the local OCD squad. They did some discreet checking and found that the information Grushev had given them panned out.

"Apparently he'd been employed at one of the uranium enrichment plants in the Ural Mountains. He told them he'd been smuggling out uranium 235 for more than nine months. He was in debt up to his ears and had a family to support, and a sick wife. So when someone came to him with a deal, he took it with both hands. Grushev told the cops that he brought out the uranium, handed it over and got hard cash. No questions asked."

"I would've figured that the Russians would have some kind of routine inspection in place," Bolan said.

"They have, but it's loose to say the least. The irony is that Grushev was an inspector at the plant where he worked. He was able to cover his tracks by altering records. It would've come out eventually, he knew that, but by then he would've been able to have taken care of his family. That was the way he saw it."

"His employers had different ideas?"

Brognola nodded. "He made his final delivery the night he was shot. He'd been expecting a big payoff. It turned out to be bigger than he thought. Somebody cut him to pieces with a 9 mm Uzi and left him for dead."

"Tidying up loose ends," Bolan said. "They didn't want anyone alive who might be able to finger them."

"I guess so, but Grushev did stay alive long enough to tell his side of the story."

"Who was he dealing with?"

"He made contact with three people each time. A Russian did all the talking. Grushev had only one good piece of evidence on one of the other two. He heard him speaking to the Russian. Grushev couldn't understand him, but he did say that he spoke with an American accent."

Bolan digested that last piece of information as they left the hotel and picked up the big Fed's car. As he wheeled his way through the traffic, Brognola let the silence hang.

"What else have you got, Hal?" Bolan finally asked.

"Aaron did a sweep of major and minor Intelligence agencies, here and in Europe. He came up with a number of isolated slices that make up a pretty tempting pie.

"It looks like we have a client, unknown at the moment, who's negotiating with a Russian named Petrochenko to provide them with the raw material to construct a crude, but usable nuclear device."

"But we don't know who, or why they want such a device?"

"The fact that an American's involved doesn't necessarily mean the device will be used in the U.S.,"

Brognola said, "but we can't rule out that possibility, either."

"This has been in the cards for a while," Bolan said. "Terrorists, blackmailers, some group with a grievance, getting its hands on a bomb small enough to be moved wherever they want it. If one group gets away with it, there could be an epidemic of such attacks."

"That's what the top brass feels. The difficulty is pinning down a small group able to put up the stakes and move about at will. It needs your kind of input, Mack. By the time government agencies get into gear, we could be counting the dead and wondering how many are going to go down with radiation poisoning."

"I need a starting point, Hal."

"You already have it. Vasily Petrochenko. According to the OCD, he's one of the new breed of criminals taking advantage of Russia's freer society. The bottom line has him as an out-and-out gangster, but a very organized and ruthless one. Clever as well. He always covers his tracks and has the money and clout to wriggle out from under anything. The guy has been involved in drugs and the black market on a grand scale. These days he's into arms dealing, buying and selling anything he can get his hands on. Word is that he's moving in higher circles now and wants to leave all the small-time stuff behind. The

OCD can't prove it, but they have Petrochenko down for Grushev's murder. It was done in the style he's noted for."

Brognola pulled out a photograph from his inside pocket and passed it to Bolan. It was a head and shoulders shot, taken from a larger print, that showed a lean, hollow-cheeked man with heavy-lidded eyes behind spectacles.

"This is Dr. Ralph Semple. His speciality is nuclear weapons. He used to work for the U.S. government before cutbacks lost him his job. Since then he's fallen heavily into debt and become a bitter man who resents what happened to him. Plus he has a drinking problem."

"Where does Semple fit into the picture?"

"Interpol was doing some discreet surveillance on Petrochenko during a trip he made to France as a favor to the OCD. They followed him around, taking photographs. When copies came to us, we saw that one of them was of our good doctor in conversation with an American named Mason Sheppard."

"Sheppard? That name sounds familiar."

"Ex-CIA. He used to be their man on the Afghanistan-Russian border, and he knows the country like the back of his hand. Sheppard had a big fallout with the Company some years back. He really made his feelings known. Rumor has it Langley sent out a team to bring him in, or terminate him. It appears Sheppard reversed the action. Since then he's been free-lancing. For the past eighteen months he's been linked with Vasily Petrochenko.''

"Anything else?"

"I have a contact for you in the OCD. He's one of the officers involved in the Grushev case, a Captain Danovitch. But your first stop is Scotland. Mason Sheppard is arriving there the day after tomorrow. It's a place on the northeast coast, way off the beaten track. We're certain he isn't going there for his health, especially not with Ray Kasden, his old buddy from his CIA days as a traveling companion. Kasden's a specialist. His talent is killing people. He was trained as a hit man. Now he gets paid for doing it.''

2

Scotland

Mason Sheppard stepped out of the hotel. He turned
up the collar of his coat and hurried across the street
to where a car was parked at the curb. Bolan had
spotted the vehicle's arrival a couple of minutes earlier. The moment Sheppard got inside, the car eased
away from the curb and drove off along the narrow
main street, heading out of the village.

Bolan started his own engine, slipped the car into
gear and began to tail Sheppard's vehicle. At first
he'd thought that Sheppard's driver was Ray Kasden, but it was more likely that the driver was simply that—a wheelman-bodyguard, there to protect
Sheppard. Kasden was probably already at the
meeting place, waiting for his target to arrive.

After a couple of miles the minor road they traveled merged with a highway. There was more traffic
and Bolan allowed a small van to pass him before he
fell in. He was easily able to keep Sheppard's car in

sight. Driving was slow due to the winding road and the continuing rain.

Ten minutes later Sheppard's car took a left turn. So did the small van. Bolan eased back farther, still keeping Sheppard in sight.

Outside a small village Sheppard's car turned left again, over a stone bridge. The van drove straight on. Bolan coasted to the turn. Sheppard's car had curved around to the right, onto a road signposting a local sight-seeing area. Gaining the bend, Bolan saw that it was a single track road, with regular passing areas cut into the grass verges. He slowed almost to a crawl, letting Sheppard's car disappear from sight around a couple of bends.

The rain stopped a couple of minutes later. The clouds drifted away, and a pale sun shone on the thick stands of pine that bordered the road. A narrow river ran below the level of the road.

Up ahead the road opened out onto a flat area bounded on one side by the river and a waterfall. On Bolan's left was a wide parking lot, large enough to hold a number of touring coaches as well as private cars. At the far end of the lot was a building constructed from pine, containing a tourist shop, cafeteria and information center. Branching off from the parking lot were signposted paths leading into the forest.

Bolan parked his car, checking that the Beretta was snug in its shoulder holster before climbing out of the vehicle and locking the door. He had already pinpointed Sheppard's car.

Then he saw Sheppard himself. He was standing next to a slim, balding man who was wearing a blue raincoat. Sheppard seemed to be doing most of the talking, while his companion kept shaking his head. Sheppard suddenly stopped speaking. He nodded to his companion, then gestured toward the forest, taking the man's arm. Together they headed along the path into the thickness of the trees.

Bolan went after them. As he approached Sheppard's car, he saw the driver was still seated behind the wheel.

He'd gone beyond the car, when he heard the crunch of gravel as the man stepped out, caught the click of the door being closed quietly. Bolan carried on, his ears tuned to the movement of the man behind him.

The canopy of tall pines closed over Bolan's head. The forest was quiet, the only distinct sound the drip of rain from the branches. The surroundings were in deep shadow, leaves covering the forest floor.

Bolan could see Sheppard and his companion a good distance ahead, deep in conversation. He saw them take a turn in the path.

The steady tread of the man behind Bolan became a sudden rush, growing louder as the guy closed in. The Executioner waited until the last moment, then turned on his heel, bringing up his right arm and smashing it into the throat of his pursuer. The impact lifted the big man off his feet and drove him to the ground with a heavy thump. He rolled as he struck the earth, his solid bulk surprisingly agile. He gained his feet in seconds, then launched himself at Bolan.

At the last moment, the Executioner caught the cold glint of a knife. The big man curved it in low, slashing at Bolan's stomach. The soldier dodged, barely avoiding the tip of the blade. He kicked out with the toe of his left shoe. It struck the man's knife hand, hard enough to loosen his grip and send the weapon spinning off into the thick undergrowth.

The driver lunged forward, arms extended. He caught one of Bolan's shoulders, his fingers digging in. He yanked the Executioner closer, then swung with his other hand to connect with Bolan's face. The blow glanced off the side of the soldier's jaw. He rolled with the impact, then countered, landing his fist directly on the man's nose. The sound of the bone crunching was followed by a gush of blood. The hardman stood frozen for a second, and Bolan used the break to lean in closer and deliver a powerful palm jab under his jaw. The man's head snapped back. The Executioner delivered a hard, sharp jab with his left fist that rammed his knuckles into his adversary's exposed larynx. This time he went down and stayed down, gagging as he tried to get his breath.

Bolan turned on his heel and took up the trail again, eyes scanning the way ahead as he sought to target Sheppard and his companion, ears straining to pick up any sound that might draw him in the right direction. He heard nothing except the drip of rainwater from the foliage.

He moved on, at the same time loosening the holstered Beretta, finger easing under the trigger guard.

He came to a split in the path and scanned the ground, but there were no footprints to indicate which path Sheppard had taken. The left fork appeared to continue in a wide curve that would bring walkers back to the starting point, providing them with a short trek through the forest. The right path looked as if it pushed deeper into the forest. Bolan opted for this route.

Within a few minutes he knew he'd been correct. The path wound its way through denser stands of trees, and much of the natural light was cut off. The rain started again, and chill droplets began to fall from the trees.

From ahead came the sound of someone blundering through the undergrowth. Bolan increased his pace, his eyes searching the way ahead. He pulled out the Beretta, flicked off the safety and made sure the weapon was on single-shot mode.

The noise grew louder, and a man shouted out in alarm.

The Executioner broke into a run, dodging trees and tangled foliage. He almost passed the struggling figure. It was the flash of color, the man's blue raincoat, that caught Bolan's eye. He looked down the slope to where the man was trying to climb the slippery bank. The rain had slicked the surface, making footholds difficult.

Bolan recognized the man as the one who'd entered the forest with Sheppard.

Sheppard himself was nowhere in sight.

The man paused as Bolan appeared. When he saw the gun he yelled, "For God's sake! Don't shoot me!"

"Give me your hand," Bolan said. He crouched, leaned down the slope and reached out with his free hand.

The man hesitated, then lunged for the outstretched hand. His fingers made contact with Bolan's and curled to get a better grip.

At that moment there was a sudden eruption from the side of the man's chest. His coat blew out, shreds of cloth mingling with the bloody flesh driven from the wound. A look of surprise washed over his face, and his mouth opened in silent protest. A second shot followed, the bullet emerging just above the first, throwing the stricken man against the slope, his body jerking.

Bolan hadn't heard any shots, and he recognized the style of a professional hit man.

He knew that Ray Kasden was somewhere close by, hidden by the tangled greenery, armed with a silenced weapon.

"You have to stop him," the wounded man said.

"Do you mean Sheppard?" Bolan asked. He crouched beside the man, aware of the heavy flow of blood from his wounds. "Why?"

"The bomb casing. I completed it, but I couldn't give it to him. I realized it was wrong, what he was doing."

The man fumbled inside his coat, dragging out a worn leather wallet that he pushed into Bolan's hand.

"He'll ship it out of the country if you don't stop him." The man fell silent, his eyes open.

Bolan leaned in and checked his pulse. There was nothing; the man was dead.

Bolan stood slowly and scanned the area. He couldn't see much—just the trees and dripping foliage. He doubted that Kasden was still around. The assassin would've left the scene the moment he'd laid down his deadly fire. The sooner he vacated the area, the easier it would be to cover his tracks and avoid capture.

Back on the path, Bolan leathered the Beretta, then pocketed the man's wallet to check later. He retraced his steps through the forest, keeping a watchful eye open for the heavy he'd tangled with. When he reached the scene of their encounter, he wasn't surprised to find him gone. Sheppard probably had found him on his way out of the forest and helped him back to the parked car.

When Bolan emerged into the parking lot he saw that Sheppard's car was gone. He returned to his own vehicle, started the engine and allowed it to tick over while he checked the wallet.

He found cash, a couple of credit cards and a driver's license. The man's name was Andrew Greigson. The address on the license showed that he was from a small town some miles up the coast. There was also a business card that stated that Greigson ran a small metal foundry and workshop. It gave the same address as that on the license.

Bolan rolled the car out of the parking lot and down the narrow road.

If Sheppard had been dealing with Greigson, there was only one reason why. Greigson had spoken of a bomb casing. That would be the outer shell to contain the uranium-235 core for a nuclear device. It was looking more likely that Brognola had been correct about a rogue bomb being built. Even a small device needed manufactured items. They were not the kinds of thing that could be purchased off the shelf, so the services of a small, high-standard metal worker would be needed.

Greigson seemed to have been that man, until he had a crisis of conscience and refused to hand over the manufactured item to Sheppard. Greigson had signed his own death warrant. There was no way that Sheppard would leave him alive, not when he could identify the man who'd asked him to build a casing for a nuclear bomb.

Bolan guessed that Greigson had the casing at his workshop, which was probably where Sheppard was headed.

If the man got his hands on it, and shipped it out of the country, then Bolan's mission still had a long way to go.

3

Bolan drove through the rain, heading for the highway and Greigson's address. He drove as fast as the wet road allowed, conscious of the fact that Sheppard had a good lead on him.

A man was already dead and the mission was barely off the runway. Bolan regretted Greigson's death. The man might have been able to furnish Bolan with more information. There were questions he needed answered.

It was possible that Greigson might not have known anything about Sheppard's plans for the nuclear device. His job might have been simply to build the casing, his association with Sheppard ending there. Or had the man been privy to the details of Sheppard's plan? Bolan thought that unlikely.

The nuclear device would be constructed from any number of separate components. To tell everyone involved its intended use would jeopardize the entire operation. It was more probable that the end use of the device was a closely guarded secret, known only to a select few.

Which made Bolan's task all that much harder.

He reached the junction with the main road and pulled over to the side while he checked out his map of the local area. He located the small fishing village where Greigson had lived. It lay some twenty miles north. Bolan put the car into gear and moved off.

The rainfall became heavier. The road was awash in sections, adding more time to Bolan's journey. It took him more than an hour to cover the distance. He drove into the village, and, after getting directions from a store owner, he followed the coast road until he spotted the turnoff. Indicated by a weathered sign. The sign bore Greigson's name above that of the company he'd operated. Bolan drove on a few yards, then stopped. He climbed out of the car and scanned the layout of the place.

A tarred track led down to a stone house. Behind the house stood a low, sturdy building, with a few other smaller storage sheds scattered about. Bolan saw that the door to the main building stood open, swinging in the wind that accompanied the steady downpour. There were no vehicles in sight.

Bolan searched for any sign of movement but felt he wasn't going to detect any. Sheppard was probably long gone. The man, aware that someone was on his tail, would have moved quickly, driving directly to Greigson's place to remove the bomb casing and move on.

Bolan returned to the car and climbed in, wiping the rain from his face. He drove through an open gate down toward the house and parked some distance from it. The front door had been forced, and splints of wood lay on the ground.

He took out the Beretta and held it ready as he eased through the door. Silence greeted him at first, then as his ears became accustomed to the atmosphere, he picked up the solid tick of a clock. He saw it as he moved into the hallway, a tall, stately grandfather clock, its wood casing highly polished. He walked on, aware that he was leaving wet prints on the carpeting.

He peered into the first room, which was fitted out as an office. A big wooden desk faced the door, and shelves lined the walls. Someone had ransacked the place. Files and drawers had been opened, and their contents lay strewed across the floor. Someone had been looking for something in a hurry, and hadn't cared about the mess he'd made.

Greigson wouldn't have kept the bomb casing in his office, but he might have retained any paperwork generated by the contract, maybe even information on how to contact Sheppard.

Sheppard would have needed to make sure there was no way anyone could trace him.

Bolan turned to leave the office, deciding he needed to check the workshop area. As he neared the door he noticed wet marks other than his own on the carpet. That they hadn't yet soaked into the floor covering indicated that the perpetrator hadn't been long gone.

Maybe someone was still inside the house.

Bolan eased around the office door, ears tuned to pick up any sound that might indicate a presence.

He heard nothing, except the tick of the big clock against the wall. His gaze passed across it, and he caught a flicker of movement reflected in its polished surface.

He ducked, arching his upper body around, hearing the sudden intake of breath as his assailant powered himself for an attack.

Whirling, Bolan saw the man let loose with a length of steel pipe, aiming it at his head. The Executioner's lightning-fast move took him below the savage strike and the pipe barely brushed his hair, connecting instead with the casing of the clock. He threw himself at his attacker, driving the man against the wall, winding him. He then swept up his right elbow in a short, savage blow that slammed against the man's jaw.

As the guy tried to wield the pipe again, Bolan drove the edge of the Beretta against the man's skull, hard and fast, so that he slipped to his knees, the steel pipe dropping from his grip. With one more bone-snapping blow to his jaw, his opponent fell facedown on the carpet. Bolan turned him over. Despite the blood that covered the man's face, Bolan recognized him as the heavy he'd tangled with in the forest.

The Executioner frisked him, emptying his pockets. He came up with a stubby pistol and two spare magazines, as well as a slim switchblade knife, keys on a ring and a battered leather wallet that appeared to be stuffed with money and cards. There was also an airline ticket and a passport. He scooped up the stuff and shoved it into his pockets. He used the unconscious man's belt to tie his hands tightly behind his back.

Bolan left the house, crossed the yard and entered the workshop, which was equipped with an array of metal-turning machinery and a computer-controlled cutter. The walls were lined with racks holding tools. At the far end was an area containing a computer that Greigson had obviously used to work out his designs, and a number of files. They, too, had been ransacked, and papers were strewn across the floor.

He surveyed the mess. He knew there was little point in continuing his search. Sheppard would have made certain there was nothing left to connect him with Greigson.

He was about to turn away when something caught his eye. It was a blinking red light. Bolan took a longer look and froze.

A familiar shape was nestled between stacks of files. He'd seen too many—and planted a few himself—not to recognize an explosive compound, and that timer was counting down the seconds with remorseless efficiency.

Bolan flung himself along the workshop, muscles taut as he targeted the exit.

He reached the doorway and plunged through it into the chill of the rain.

Even from a distance of twenty feet, he felt the shock wave, followed by the stunning boom of the explosion. He was hurled across the ground and came crashing down hard. He felt the heat, then debris rained around him, some slamming into him.

Before his ears had stopped pounding, a second explosion rent the air and Greigson's house vanished before his eyes. He covered his head with his arms as the ground shook and more debris crashed around him.

He struggled to his feet and was almost upright when a flying chunk of debris struck him across the back of the head. He pitched facedown on the ground, this time oblivious to the noise and destruction around him.

4

"Have you collected the item?"

"Yes, I have it with me now," Mason Sheppard replied on the other end of the line.

"And the arrangements?"

"On target. We should be able to move the item within the next forty-eight hours. I'd like to do it as soon as possible, though."

"You sound concerned."

"There was a problem."

"Go on."

"Someone followed me to my meet with Greigson and turned up later at his workshop," Sheppard said.

"This someone, I presume he was dealt with?"

"I left Gage behind to destroy Greigson's place so there wouldn't be anything to identify us."

"But?"

"Gage didn't come back."

"Who was this man?"

"I don't know. I didn't hear him speak, so I can only guess. He could have been British or American, but he's most probably from one of the security agencies."

"Are we compromised? Will this interfere with the operation?"

"I believe we're still safe and the item is secure," Sheppard assured his caller. "This man is running on borrowed time. He was just lucky with the Greigson meet, but there's nothing to guide him any further."

"Can you be certain Gage hasn't told him anything?"

"Okay, so I'm not one hundred percent certain, but I know that if he turns up again we can handle him."

"You better make sure you do deal with him. It might be wise to take the offensive, so don't wait for him to come to you. Send in some of your people to stop him before he becomes a real threat. Hire some local help if you have to. We have the connections and the money. I want you to wipe him out, Mason."

"Leave it to me. How are the other items progressing?"

"We're on schedule, but I'll only be satisfied once everything is brought together."

"If I can keep to my timetable I should be with you in a few days."

"Good. Keep me informed."

There was a click in Sheppard's ear as the connection was broken. He stared at the receiver for a moment before replacing it. He looked around the cramped office, feeling confined in the cluttered space. The room reeked of oil. The walls were hung with a collection of old, faded calendars, and sagging shelves held volumes of well-used manuals relating to the marine business.

A knock at the door caused Sheppard to turn. It opened to admit an overweight man in stained coveralls and a thick wool sweater, wiry gray hair sticking out from under his cap. He thrust out a big hand, offering Sheppard a mug of steaming tea.

"You all fixed up now, mate?" Tam McClain asked.

"Yeah."

"I'm ready anytime. Just say the word, lad, and we'll have your package across the water before you know it."

"It could be sooner than later," Sheppard said. "There's been a change of plan."

"Aye, that's the way life tends to go. Like I said, just give the nod and we're off."

McClain took a swallow from his own mug, smacking his lips noisily.

"Same destination I take it?"

Sheppard nodded.

"The only reason I ask is so I don't have to plot a new course at the last minute."

"No problem," Sheppard said. He took a sip from his mug. The tea was scalding and strong enough to melt steel bars. The only saving grace was the generous amount of whiskey McClain had added.

McClain grinned. "I bet you've never tasted tea with such a bite."

"Damn right there, McClain."

The Scot had been recommended to Sheppard by a business acquaintance who dealt in contraband: guns, drugs, illegal immigrants—anything that brought in money, and all of it unlawful. Sheppard had dealt with the man a few times before, so he trusted him when told that Tam McClain was dependable. Sheppard had no complaints on that score; the man had delivered up to now.

The next phase in the operation had already been planned, down to the smallest detail, but now they'd been changed. Only Sheppard knew about the changes. As far as McClain was concerned, the original plan still stood. He'd been contracted to take the bomb casing across the sea to Stavanger, Norway, where it would be collected by the crew of an ex-Soviet submarine. The boat was able to carry out its illicit operations safely, in and out of Russian waters, due to the crew's knowledge of the undersea lanes. The submarine pickup was still on, which meant that McClain would still believe he was carrying the illicit cargo. In the meantime Sheppard would be shipping out the real casing by a different route.

McClain might be an expert at avoiding detection on the high seas, but there was always a first time, Sheppard thought. They couldn't afford to be too careful.

Sheppard realized that his decision to stay around Greigson's place after leaving Gage to handle things had been worth it. He had seen the stranger arrive and later had witnessed him being knocked down by the blast from one of Gage's bombs. Sheppard had slipped away from the place just as the local cops had rolled in, alerted by the powerful explosions.

He took another swallow of McClain's potent brew, then placed the mug on the cluttered desk.

"I've got to go. I'll be back later, and we'll go over the final details."

"Aye," McClain said, busy pouring a further tot of whiskey into his half-drained tea mug. "See you later, laddie."

Sheppard left the office and walked down the steep wooden steps to the dock. He turned up the collar of his coat against the rain as he headed toward his parked car. Like his office, McClain's boatyard was a mess. Littered with the paraphernalia of boats and tackle, the ground underfoot was dirty and oily. An assortment of craft in various degrees of repair were moored in the choppy water. Out beyond the small harbor, the North Sea looked gray and dismal, rain scudding over the whitecaps of the running tide.

Reaching his car, Sheppard unlocked it and slid in. He picked up the car phone and punched in a number. A man finally answered.

"You were recommended to me by Craig Pearson."

"Are you Sheppard?"

"Yeah. I have a job for you. I need someone taken care of."

"How do you want him dealt with? A shock to the system, or a more permanent solution?"

"This guy isn't the kind who'll take advice to back off," Sheppard said, "so I go for the second option."

"Fair enough."

"I'm pretty certain this guy is an American, and I'm guessing he's staying fairly local. He's driving a dark blue car. Right now he's probably with the local police, but I think he'll be back on the street soon enough."

"We'll find him. How do I get in touch with you?"

"Do you know Tam McClain?"

"Yes."

"Through him, then."

"Consider the problem taken care of."

Sheppard cut the connection and punched in another number. It was answered after the first ring.

"Kas?"

"You took your damn time," Ray Kasden said.

"Is everything all right?"

"I guess," Kasden replied. "I'll be out of here in an hour. Is there something I should know?"

"Yeah. The guy who tangled with Gage showed up at Greigson's place. It looks like he tangled with Gage again. When the place blew Gage went with it, but the guy got out."

"Damn, I hate loose ends. Where is he now?"

"Probably up to his ears in trouble. I stayed around long enough to see the local cops turn up. He was flattened by the blast from the house."

"If he has connections, he'll get out."

"Maybe, but it'll be awhile. It'll give us time to move the merchandise and get the hell out of this backwater ourselves. In the meantime I've arranged a welcoming committee for him when he does show. Some local talent is going to handle him for us."

Kasden laughed. "You do like your little games, Mason."

"I just want this guy out of the picture. There's enough to handle without some government snoop shadowing me."

"I'll see you back at base in a few days."

Sheppard hung up. He put the car into gear and drove out of the boatyard. Before he did anything else he had to check that a certain item was secure. Only then would he give Tam McClain his instructions.

5

Detective Sergeant Alex Maitland walked along the stone-flagged passage, dreading the moment he would have to reenter the interview room.

He stopped outside the door, taking a deep breath before turning the handle. He opened the door, nodding briefly to the police constable standing against the wall.

The interview room was small and square, with a single barred window set high up in the stone wall. A light suspended from the ceiling illuminated a wooden table, littered with empty tea mugs and an overflowing ashtray. There were three wooden chairs. Only one was occupied at the moment, by a man who called himself Mike Belasko.

Maitland had spent the past few hours interviewing him. Belasko had been polite, but he hadn't given the detective a single useful piece of information. It was obvious that he was used to being questioned by the police. He knew how to avoid being drawn into any kind of admission, content to wait for a response from the people he'd contacted when he'd been allowed to make a telephone call.

Half an hour earlier, Maitland had been summoned from the interview room to take a call himself. It had been from his chief constable. In no uncertain terms the chief had instructed Maitland to drop his questioning of Belasko. The chief had received his orders, and he was passing them down the chain of command.

Belasko had immunity, the kind that stretched all the way back to Whitehall in London. Maitland had been about to argue his case, when the chief cut in.

"There's more to this, Maitland, than either you or I know. The word is we don't ask questions, we simply turn Belasko loose. It seems the man has a job to do, so we offer him any assistance he might need."

Maitland sat down. He took out his pack of cigarettes and lit one.

"It appears that you have friends who are able to move mountains, Belasko. I've just come from a chat with my chief. His orders, and now my orders, are to turn you loose, with no questions and no charges. You're free to go whenever you want."

Bolan could understand Maitland's frustration. He'd been told to disregard the fact that Bolan had been linked to two violent deaths. The detective had to open the door and allow him to walk away, free and clear, with no explanations. It wasn't the first time officialdom had given the Executioner his freedom, and it wouldn't be the last.

"I know you'd like to lock me up and throw away the key," Bolan said. "I don't blame you, and the fact I'm going to walk out of here is going to tie you in knots. I understand that, too. But I don't have an easy answer for you, Maitland. I have my reasons for what I'm doing. I'm on your side, but the people I'm after understand only one thing. Direct action, and that's the only way I can stop them."

"And what are they doing, Belasko? Can you tell me that?"

"If I knew, I'd give you as much of the picture as I could. Right now I'm following up on information so thin you can see through it. It led me to Greigson, but not soon enough to stop him from being murdered. I went to his foundry, but the opposition was ahead of me there, as well. They took something Greigson had made for them and boobytrapped his house and workshop. One of them stayed behind and we tangled. I got out just in time."

"Why would they want to destroy Greigson's place?"

"Probably to make certain they eliminated any evidence that might link them to Greigson."

Maitland studied the American. "What kind of people are they?"

"These are hard men, Maitland. They kill and destroy for a living. They'll wipe out anyone or anything that gets in their way."

"Are we talking terrorists?"

"Could be. We don't have that close an identification on them yet."

"You said earlier that you believed Greigson had been killed by an assassin, a hit man, as you Americans would say. Why a man like Greigson? You have to realize, Belasko, that linking Greigson to a professional killer sounds like some TV drama to me."

"It's not the usual kind of crime you get up here, I guess."

Maitland forced a smile. "Oh, we get our murders, but they'll be the domestic types, usually, not hit men and booby-trapped houses."

He stood. "Let's go through to my office."

Settled in Maitland's cramped office, Bolan watched as the detective took a cardboard box from a cupboard. The box contained Bolan's personal effects, including the shoulder rig and the Beretta.

"Impressive weapon," Maitland said.

Bolan took off his jacket, eased on the shoulder rig, then holstered the pistol. He pocketed his wallet and other effects.

"There were also these," Maitland said, holding up a buff envelope. "From Gage, the man you fought with at Greigson's place?"

"Yes."

"Will they help you?"

Bolan shrugged. "I haven't had a chance to check them over yet."

"We did. There's a receipt here from a hotel in Stavanger, Norway, dated a few days ago and a parking ticket from the same place. According to the man's passport, prior to that he was in Russia. Gage moved around a great deal."

Bolan studied Gage's passport. He was a U.S. citizen, born in Boston. At the time of his death, he'd been thirty-six years old. His profession, according to his passport, was professional photographer.

"I met up with him twice," Bolan said, "and I never saw him with a camera."

Maitland settled back in his chair.

"Where do you go from here?"

"Back to my hotel. I'll contact my people and have them run a detailed check into Gage's background, who he knew, the circles he moved in. I'll pick it up from there and try to figure out where Norway and Russia come into the picture."

Bolan slid Gage's belongings back into the envelope.

"I wish you luck, Belasko." Maitland stood. "I have a feeling you're going to need it."

"Thanks," Bolan said. "Is my car here?"

"In the yard behind the station. I'll walk down with you."

The rain had stopped, but the sky threatened more rain before long.

Bolan climbed into the vehicle and fired up the engine. He swung the car around and drove onto the main street of the small town, picking up the signs that would get him back on the road south.

He linked up with the main road a mile farther on and settled back in his seat, allowing the car to pick up speed. The road was quiet, with little traffic in sight, which was why Bolan noticed the mud-streaked Volvo some three hundred yards behind him. The road offered the other car easy passing space, but the driver made no attempt to close the distance.

Ten minutes later the position was the same. When Bolan dropped his speed, the Volvo did the same, increasing its speed when the soldier stepped on the gas.

The Executioner had picked up a tail.

6

A turn appeared up ahead. Bolan left it to the last moment, then swung the wheel hard. His car slid on the wet surface of the road, and he almost overshot his mark. He regained control and trod hard on the gas pedal. The car hurtled along the narrow road, overhanging trees slapping at the windshield. He moved too close to the side and the wheels dropped onto the muddy shoulder. He felt the vehicle lurch against the sloping bank and he fought the wheel, pulling the car back into the center of the road.

He spotted the Volvo in the rearview mirror. The big car was coming on without letup. The road curved ahead, and Bolan rounded the bend. A gout of dark mud flew up, splashing the windshield. He flicked on the wipers, jamming his thumb against the water-spray button. For a few seconds, his vision was blocked by the mud and water across the glass. By the time the wipers had cleared the surface, it was too late for him to avoid the deep pothole in the road.

Bolan felt the hard slam as the right front suspension hit the road. The steering wheel was wrenched from his grip, and the car slewed across the narrow road and plowed headlong into the sloping bank. It came to an abrupt halt, the engine stalling.

The soldier didn't waste time trying to restart the car. He pushed open his door and climbed out.

He could hear the approaching Volvo, the engine roaring as the driver pushed it hard. It would be in sight within seconds.

He reached under his jacket and pulled out the Beretta. He flicked off the safety, setting the fire-selector switch to 3-round bursts.

He'd taken no more than two steps from the car when the Volvo came around the bend. The driver slammed on the brakes and brought the vehicle to a halt.

The front passenger door flew open and a heavy-set man hauled himself out of the car. He was dragging a long-barreled shotgun behind him, and he swung it to his shoulder the moment he saw Bolan.

The Executioner had anticipated some kind of action from his pursuers, and he was already taking evasive action. He heard the shotgun's heavy blast as he dived across the road and shoulder-rolled through the wet grass. Pellets scoured the road surface in his wake, a couple of them catching the heel of one shoe.

Harsh voices rang out, followed by the crash of heavy boots.

Bolan turned on his stomach, half rising, the Beretta already tracking in on the closest of his attackers. His finger stroked the trigger and the gunner was halted in his tracks, the front of his chest opening up into a bloody mess. He staggered drunkenly, before pitching sideways onto the ground.

Someone opened up with another shotgun off to Bolan's left. The blast tore through the foliage, sending shredded leaves and branches into the air. The hit was feet away from Bolan who had already moved, taking aim again. He dropped the second would-be killer with a tri-burst that blew away most of his throat. The man went down, his weapon abandoned, his hands clasped around his pulsing wound.

Under cover of the thick foliage that flanked the soft shoulder, Bolan swiftly moved back along the road until he was level with the parked Volvo. All the doors were open and Bolan could see two more armed men, weapons up, scouring the area. There was a third person behind the wheel, shouting orders to his accomplices.

One of the armed men moved to the rear of the car, while the other skirted Bolan's stalled vehicle.

The Executioner was about to make his own move when the driver climbed out of the car, cradling a sawed-off shotgun under one arm. He fished cartridges out of a pocket as he scanned the area. He broke the shotgun's action and stuffed two shells into place.

Before he could close the action, Bolan leveled the Beretta.

"Close that and I'll drop you where you stand."

Bolan whispered his warning so that only the man would hear it.

The man turned in Bolan's direction.

"You won't get out of this alive, you bastard," he said. "Not when two of my boys are done for. You're dead."

He snapped the shotgun shut and swiveled the barrels at Bolan.

The Beretta coughed its 9 mm burst. The gunner was nailed against the side of the Volvo, one of the slugs boring through him to shatter the window behind him.

Bolan spun on his heel, picking up the moving figure of the gunman at the front of the Volvo.

They fired together.

The shotgun's blast took out the windshield.

Bolan's slugs missed their mark by a fraction, allowing the man to duck out of sight on the far side of the car.

The man at the rear of the Volvo found himself distracted by the roar of an approaching car. It swept into sight, heading directly for him. He fired his shotgun, the rounds starring the windshield. He turned and tried to get out of the way, but the car struck him a glancing blow and he was thrown across the road, arms and legs windmilling. He crashed facedown in the muddy grass.

Bolan sprinted around the Volvo. As he reached the far side, he met the surviving gunner. The man had already decided that the new car on the scene couldn't touch him, so his priority was Bolan. His thinking was right, but his timing was off.

As the Executioner and the gunner came face-to-face, there was a split second as each man weighed up his chances of survival.

Then Bolan's hand moved in a blur and the Beretta let go its deadly burst. The tri-burst caught the gunner high up in the chest, and he went over backward without a sound. His shotgun flew from his hands, describing a slow arc before it landed in a puddle of rainwater.

The Executioner ejected the spent magazine and snapped in a fresh one. As he cocked the Beretta, he heard a car door slam.

Detective Maitland lit a cigarette as he surveyed the damaged windshield of his car. He shook his head as Bolan approached.

"I'll never get the insurance to pay for that," he said.

"What are you doing here, Maitland?" Bolan asked.

"I watched you leave, then I saw that Volvo follow you. I decided maybe I should offer you some protection."

"I'm grateful," Bolan said. "What made you realize they were following me?"

"The way they acted. One of them was standing watch across the street. The minute you turned the corner he waved the Volvo in, and they followed. Of course it helped that I knew the one on watch. We've had him on file for years."

Bolan crossed to the man Maitland had hit with his car. The man was still down, but groaning loudly.

"What the hell is going on, Belasko?" Maitland said. "Just look at this mess. Dead bodies, gunfights. They'll have me down as a reckless driver. You seem to have a habit of drawing a lot of bad people out of the woodwork."

The downed man was clutching his leg, which was clearly broken. Bolan glanced at Maitland.

"You got a radio in your car?"

Maitland nodded. "I'll have them send an ambulance."

As the detective moved to his car, Bolan crouched beside the hurt gunner. The man's face was beaded with sweat.

"You could still end up like your pals," Bolan said, letting the man see the Beretta.

"Shoot me in front of a cop?" the man spit. "You're bluffing."

"Am I? He doesn't run this show. I have my own rules and I decide who lives or dies. You and your cohorts were out to kill me, so don't expect any sympathy."

"You're crazy, man. Sheppard won't let this stop him from getting to you."

"Now you've given the game away. Sheppard isn't going to be too happy about that. He should've hired professionals, not a bunch of bar flies."

"You bastard."

"At least I'm still alive and free."

The words sank in. The man's eyes flickered back and forth. He was seeking a way out, anything to save his own skin.

"I could tell you where we had to make contact."

"In exchange for what?"

"A good word to the law."

"If the information is worth it."

"Tam McClain's boatyard in Craig."

Bolan stood and walked over to Maitland.

"The ambulance and backup cars are on their way," Maitland said. He glanced at the injured man. "Has he been talking?"

"Nothing you'd be interested in," Bolan replied.

Maitland grunted. "I'm not so sure, but I get the message."

"He's expecting some kind of deal."

"Is he now?" Maitland smiled. "But he didn't tell me a damn thing, Belasko, so how can I deal?"

"Can you arrange a car for me? I need to move out pretty fast."

"I already did that. It'll be waiting when we get back to the station."

Bolan nodded. He was already thinking ahead, to a boatyard along the coast, a way for Sheppard to move his merchandise out of the country, across the North Sea, perhaps. From there it was anybody's guess, but it was a step closer to Russia and Vasily Petrochenko. It was time to make use of Brognola's contact over there, just as soon as he paid a visit to McClain's boatyard.

7

Darkness and mist reduced Mack Bolan's range of vision. It also provided cover, enabling him to breach the perimeter fence surrounding Tam McClain's boatyard.

Clad in his blacksuit, with the Beretta leathered in its shoulder rig, he slid silently through the shadows, closing on the ramshackle building that housed the repair shop, with the office and stores above.

The yard was a mess. Rotting hulls and discarded tackle were strewed everywhere. Drums of fuel and oil stood in untidy heaps. A couple of cars and a battered Toyota pickup sat parked in the area.

Lights shone from the office, and Bolan detected movement behind the grimy glass of one window. Apart from that, the yard seemed deserted.

A salvage tug rocked in the water, its idling diesel engine pulsing into the night. The vessel seemed large enough to undertake long-distance sea voyages.

A sound caught Bolan's attention. He turned in time to see a group of men exit the office and start down the flight of wooden steps that led to the ground.

As the group reached the midway point, they passed under a security light. Bolan recognized one of them from a photograph supplied by Stony Man Farm. It was Ray Kasden, and he was carrying a slim assault rifle. Two of the other men were handling a square wooden packing box between them.

Mason Sheppard was nowhere in sight.

Bolan watched them for a few moments. If the box contained what he believed it did, namely, the casing for a nuclear device, he had to initiate some kind of action quickly. He didn't have the means to destroy the item, so the only other course open to him was to attempt to hijack it.

The Toyota pickup was the vehicle closest to him. He made his way to the side of the truck and opened the driver's door. The keys were in the ignition. He checked out the interior. The floor was littered with papers and empty cigarette packages. He sifted through the mess on the dashboard, his fingers closing over a box of matches. He took them with him, screwing up a wad of paper from the floor of the pickup. He then crept to a stack of diesel drums. Using a length of flat iron pipe he found on the ground, he loosened the bung on one of the drums and allowed the fuel to spill out. The drum was full and the pungent liquid flooded out in a thick stream, splashing across the ground and running down the incline that led to the water's edge. Bolan repeated the operation with a second and third drum, until there was a steady stream of fuel running downslope.

He soaked the wad of papers with fuel, then struck a match and lit the makeshift torch. It flared, and he dropped it into the stream of liquid. The vapors ignited with a soft whoosh, and the flames shot into the air. Bolan returned to the pickup as the flames raced the length of the spilled fuel.

He yanked open the driver's door and slid across the seat, the Beretta in his left hand. He turned the ignition key and heard the engine catch. He jammed his foot on the gas and slammed the truck into gear. He swung the vehicle in a tight turn that took him across the yard on course for the group of men nearing the idling vessel.

The men had already broken apart, startled by the eruption of blazing fuel. Kasden was urging them to get the packing case onto the tug.

The hit man turned to face the pickup, snapping the rifle to his shoulder.

Bolan flicked on the headlights and the beams caught Kasden full in the face. He covered his eyes and turned his head, momentarily blinded by the glare.

The Executioner had already shifted the Beretta to his right hand. Steering the pickup with his left, he leaned out the open window and picked up Kasden in his sights.

The hit man shouldered his rifle again, this time firing quickly. Two of his slugs struck the truck's roll bar, raising sparks. Kasden shifted his aim lower.

Bolan loosed twin 3-round bursts.

Kasden lurched under the impact of the 9 mm slugs. His rifle tilted skyward as he fell to his knees.

Bolan pulled on the wheel, taking the Toyota in the direction of the pair carrying the packing case.

He might have reached them if it hadn't have been for the dark figure that appeared on the deck of the tug. The night was split apart by the heavy chatter of a large caliber automatic weapon. Bolan felt the vehicle shudder as slugs chewed into the bodywork. He heard a tire blow and felt the steering go dead. Before he could react, the speeding truck overturned. He was thrown across the seat as the Toyota slid along the ground, coming to rest with its side engulfed in the burning fuel.

Dazed, his face bloody from a gash on his forehead, Bolan fought to get his feet under him. The chatter of the machine gun filled his ears, heavy slugs tearing into the truck. He grabbed his weapon from the floor where it had fallen, then drove both feet against the windshield. The glass pebbled into pieces and he pushed his way through the opening, using the overturned truck to hide him from his adversaries. He then threw up his right arm to shield his face from the flames, and took a headlong dive away from the truck. He landed hard, rolling and coming to his feet in one fluid move.

"No damn way, you son of a bitch!"

Bolan turned, tracking with his Beretta. The bloodied figure of Kasden appeared around the rear of the truck. He clutched his bleeding side with one hand, the other bringing up the rifle.

The soldier drilled a 3-round burst into Kasden before he could close a finger around the trigger of the rifle. Bolan's aim was on target, and the trio of 9 mm tumblers carved into Kasden's throat in a burst of red, flinging him back from the truck.

Bolan broke away from the vehicle, long strides taking him through the wall of fire to behind the group of men by the tug.

The pair carrying the packing case was already hoisting it onto the vessel. One man remained on the dock, weapon up and ready, while the gunner on the tug wielded his heavy weapon, his elevated position enabling him to have a clearer view of the area.

Within moments of Bolan clearing the wall of flame, the gunner spotted him. He triggered a burst, the large-caliber slugs pounding the earth inches from the Executioner. Bolan dived away from the line of fire, his blacksuit blending in with the thicker shadows on the ground. He came up against a pile of rotting timber and stayed put while he assessed the situation.

Voices rose above the beat of the tug's engine, and Bolan heard the splash of mooring lines being dropped into the water. The tug began to ease away from the dock. It picked up speed quickly, its exterior obviously concealing powerful engines.

Bolan saw his quarry fading into the night.

He shifted his sights to the lone gunner standing on the dock. He switched the selector to single-shot mode, just as the gunner picked up the Executioner's presence and snatched at the subgun hanging by a shoulder strap.

Bolan put a single shot through the gunman's heart, punching him off his feet, over the edge of the dock and into the water.

Skirting the still burning fuel, Bolan paused beside Kasden's outstretched body. The assassin's pockets yielded nothing. He'd been a professional, not carrying anything on him before going out on assignment. There was nothing to lead the soldier back to Mason Sheppard. He headed for the boatyard office. He hugged the wall as he mounted the steps, the reloaded Beretta held before him in a two-handed grip. The office door stood ajar, a single, dim bulb shining inside. He scanned the interior. It was empty, the air still thick with the smells of tobacco smoke and overbrewed coffee from an ancient percolator. Bolan closed the door behind him as he entered the room.

He prowled the space, checking papers and inspecting charts, seeking anything that might offer some indication where Tam McClain's tug was heading.

Scattering papers off the desk, Bolan unearthed a grubby telephone. He dialed Maitland's number.

The ringing phone was answered quickly.

"Maitland, I need you to do something for me fast."

BOLAN SETTLED into the swivel chair. He was back in Detective Maitland's office, a telephone receiver pressed to his ear.

"Your flight is confirmed, Striker," Brognola said. "Aberdeen to Heathrow, then a connection directly to Moscow. You'll be met there by Captain Danovitch."

"What about my weapons?"

"Leave your handgun with the guy from the U.S. Embassy who'll be at Heathrow. Our man in Moscow has made arrangements with the Russians. They'll fix you up when you land."

"That'll have to do."

"We can't be too pushy about this, Striker. Do you realize how many strings I've had to pull with the British authorities? The sooner we get you away from there the better."

Bolan allowed himself a brief smile. There was nothing the big Fed liked better than negotiating his way out of sticky situations.

"The fact that there's been so much resistance says it all," Bolan said. "Sheppard has something to hide, and he had his people firing on all cylinders."

"Is there any more news from British customs and excise?"

"No, same as earlier. They intercepted McClain's boat and made a search. The packing case turned out to be full of scrap metal. Sheppard made a switch. He sent McClain out as a decoy while he took the genuine article out by another route."

"And McClain's still claiming he didn't know anything about it?"

"Yeah, and I believe him. Sheppard set him up to distract attention. McClain probably wouldn't have agreed to being a patsy."

"So where's Sheppard?"

"I'd say he's on his way to a rendezvous with the Russian end of the organization. If he has the casing for a nuclear bomb, the next step will be to have the thing assembled. That takes time and expertise."

"What's happening to McClain?"

"The customs people have him on possession of illegal weapons. Right now they're tearing his boatyard apart. They've been waiting their chance to turn him over for years. I don't think he's going to walk away from this one untouched."

As Bolan completed his call, the door opened and Maitland stuck his head inside the office.

"You all through?"

Bolan nodded.

"Let's go," Maitland said. "I'll drive you to the hotel. You can get cleaned up, then I'll ferry you to the chopper."

"What chopper?"

Maitland grinned. "The chief constable is so anxious to get you out of Scotland he's arranged for one of our police choppers to fly you down to Aberdeen Airport."

"That," Bolan said, "is the best thing I've heard all day."

8

The hand on his shoulder roused Bolan instantly. He stared up into the face of a British Airways flight attendant.

"Time to fasten your seat belt, Mr. Belasko. We'll be landing shortly."

Bolan nodded and sat up. He'd slept through the flight from Heathrow to Moscow, using the time to recharge his batteries. Refreshed, he peered through the window at the ground below.

Forty-five minutes later Bolan was standing in line in front of the customs counter. He still hadn't been contacted by the time he reached the desk and handed over his passport. The young Russian studied his passport, then turned and signaled someone. A second man came forward and took the passport, examining Bolan's face.

"Would you come with me, please, Mr. Belasko?"

Bolan was escorted around the desk and down a short corridor. His escort paused at a door, knocked and opened it. Bolan's passport was handed back to him as he stepped into the sparely furnished office.

It contained a desk, a couple of chairs and a dark-haired young woman dressed in pants and a jacket.

Bolan's first impression was that of youth coupled with experience. Dark eyes set in a strong, beautiful face regarded him with interest.

"I am Captain Tanya Danovitch," she said. "Did you have a good flight?"

Bolan took the hand she held out. Her grip was strong.

"Yes," he replied. "Do you want to update me on the situation?"

Danovitch smiled. "Straight to the point. You don't waste time, Mr. Belasko."

"From what I've learned about this group, they don't waste much time themselves."

"I have a car waiting outside. We can talk on the way."

"Where are we going?" Bolan asked as he followed her out of the office.

"First to the OCD area office in Moscow. You can take a look at everything we have on these people there. Then we have a long trip ahead of us to Dushanbe."

"That's in Tadzhikistan, isn't it?"

"You know my country, Mr. Belasko. You have been here before, perhaps?"

Bolan nodded. "Maybe I'll tell you about it one day."

They approached a fairly new Mercedes. Danovitch unlocked it and got in behind the wheel. Bolan dropped his bag on the rear seat and took the passenger seat. The engine burst into life, the rumble suggesting that the standard power plant had been improved upon.

"The criminal gangs we've been after use high-powered cars. If we want to catch them, we have to match their speed," she explained.

Bolan had noticed the pistol the captain wore in a shoulder rig when she took off her jacket. It was a satin-steel SIG-Sauer P-226.

"And their weaponry?"

"They are armed with the best money can buy. Arms dealing is growing here. A great deal of it comes from your country."

"Do you intend to hold that against me?"

This time she laughed. It was a soft, warm sound.

"Of course not. I'm sure that not everything in America is bad."

"We try."

Danovitch looked at him. "Mr. Belasko, I think we're going to get along," she said.

THE OCD UNIT Tanya Danovitch was attached to was based in an old building overlooking Moscow's

Byelorusskiy Station. The building was grimy and soot-streaked, a legacy of exposure to years of smoke from the locomotives that went to and from Belarus and Poland.

Danovitch parked the Mercedes in the cobbled yard that fronted the building and led Bolan inside.

His impression of the city as they'd driven through it had been fleeting, but he'd still gotten the feeling that Moscow lacked something. He'd felt it the last time he'd been here. The new freedom Russia had embraced so willingly had left the country catching its breath, not yet certain of its role at home and with the world in general. Reforms took time to implement, and a stagnant economy often took longer to haul itself into motion. All too often it was the criminal element that provided what the government couldn't offer. Russia's criminal organizations were quick to cash in on the needs of a population ready for consumerism. Along with the black-market economy came the obligatory ills—violence, murder, corruption, extortion—the sickness already eating away at the fabric of Western cultures.

The authorities fought back, which meant a beleaguered police force, and the formation of special units targeting organized crime. The Organized Crime Department was one such.

Bolan followed Danovitch up worn stone steps leading to the OCD office. When they reached the appropriate floor, she led him in through an open door.

The large high-ceilinged room was a hive of activity. There were at least eight police officers involved in a variety of tasks. Cluttered desks held computers and stacks of paper files, while bulletin boards lined the walls. In one corner fax machines hummed, and telephones rang constantly. Ashtrays brimmed over with cigarette butts, and a blue haze of smoke hung over the room.

The members of the unit, clad in plain clothes, glanced up as they entered. Some of them greeted Danovitch. The language was foreign, but Bolan could have been in a police department anywhere in the world.

"We go through here," Danovitch said.

Bolan was aware of the curious looks from the officers as he followed her.

The office Danovitch led him into was small and stuffy, and a glass partition separated it from the main room. Behind a large, scarred desk that was covered with papers and files, sat a burly man, his shirtsleeves rolled up and his tie askew. His mouth was clamped around a much chewed cigar. For a fleeting moment Bolan imagined that Hal Brognola had Russian relatives. The man stood.

"Michael Belasko, Commander Seminov," Danovitch said, introducing them.

The man stuck out a big hand. Bolan grasped it firmly.

"I appreciate your time, Commander."

Seminov nodded briefly, then gestured to a chair.

"Please," he said. As Bolan sat, Seminov glanced across at Danovitch. "Close the door, Captain, and please wait outside."

Seminov resumed his seat.

"I have spoken with your Mr. Brognola," he said. "He has detailed your involvement with Vasily Petrochenko's people in Scotland. Since you left there, information has reached us concerning the transportation of the bomb casing."

Bolan leaned forward.

"Brognola received a call from the Scottish police. It appears that they have located a private plane that was detected on its return from an illegal flight. The pilot confessed. He had taken a man fitting Mason Sheppard's description from Scotland to the coast of Norway. Sheppard had an item of cargo with him."

"Was the drop-off point near Stavanger?" Bolan asked.

Seminov nodded. "Yes."

"Sheppard and one of his people were in Stavanger before they went to Scotland," Bolan said. "Probably setting up the next stage of delivery."

"It has been suggested that a renegade submarine was used," Seminov admitted. He smiled at Bolan's expression. "I am a policeman, Mr. Belasko, not a politician. I have nothing to hide. My job is to stop crime. I am well aware of the devious methods these people use to transport their contraband." He rubbed thumb and finger together. "Money talks and buys favors here, as well as in your country.

"We may have a lead for you," he went on. He shuffled through the scattered papers on his desk, locating a dog-eared file. He opened it and took out a number of photographs and documents.

"This is Grigori Christophoulos, a known associate of Vasily Petrochenko. We lost touch with him for a while, but then we learned that he has reappeared in Dushanbe."

"Captain Danovitch mentioned Dushanbe," Bolan said, "but not the reason why we might be traveling there."

"Christophoulos is a trader in many kinds of illegal goods and services," Seminov stated. "He has very good contacts in Tadzhikistan."

"Does Petrochenko have any connection with the area?"

Seminov shrugged. "We haven't been able to confirm anything. It is a long way from Moscow, and communication in our country isn't always reliable."

"It's something to work on," Bolan said.

"This is an unusual assignment for my department. We are an independent unit within the OCD. That is why we are based here, away from the day-to-day routine. Our work takes us farther from Moscow than any other unit. Dushanbe is a long way, even for us, but you are in good hands. Captain Danovitch is extremely versatile."

Seminov produced more documentation from his drawers, which he passed to Bolan.

"You will find travel visas in there. Official police visas. Travel within Russia can still be difficult, but these should help you, as will being with Danovitch. Once you reach Dushanbe it will be necessary for you to play it by ear."

Bolan nodded. "I understand, Commander. This is a difficult assignment, as you are aware. The fewer people who know what we're looking for the better."

"Mr. Brognola explained the situation as far as he was allowed to. I was able to read between the lines. The theft of the uranium took place in Russia, so we must accept responsibility for that. I also realize that we must be careful. I leave it to you how much the captain is told."

Seminov pulled open a drawer and took out a wrapped package. He handed it to Bolan.

"I managed to arrange this for you."

Bolan opened the package and took out a SIG-Sauer P-226 and a shoulder holster. There were also a number of extra magazines.

"I appreciate that, Commander," he said.

"Good luck," Seminov said. "Captain Danovitch will take you to your hotel. Your flight to Dushanbe leaves in the morning."

THE MOSCOW NOVOTEL WAS built along modern European lines. Bolan's room had been arranged via Brognola, through the OCD. Danovitch, showing her ID, insured a smooth passage for Bolan.

"You didn't have to pull rank," Bolan said casually as they were escorted to the elevators.

She glanced at him. "You are a guest in my country, Mr. Belasko. Russia isn't full of savages. We know how to be civil."

Bolan realized he had touched a nerve.

Once they were inside his room, with the door closed, Bolan turned to her.

"I apologize. I didn't mean to insult you, or your country."

She held his gaze, then after a few moments she relented.

"My father always told me I took offense too easily."

"What did he do?"

"He was a police officer."

"How does he feel about you following in his footsteps?"

"He's dead. He was killed three years ago by drug dealers. People like Grigori Christophoulos killed him because he got too close to their operation. They waited for him to come home one night and machine gunned his car."

"Those people don't play by civilized rules," Bolan said. "It's the difference between us and them, and why the only way to deal with them is on their terms."

"You are a strange one, but I think I could get to like you."

"So why don't we make a start over dinner tonight? I don't like the idea of eating alone."

The captain smiled. "Such an offer would be hard to refuse," she said.

Dushanbe

THE FLIGHT FROM MOSCOW was long and uncomfortable. Internal flights in Russia were what Bolan termed basic. He realized that Danovitch's insistence on bringing along bottled water and food wasn't as odd as it first appeared. During the interminable hours of the flight, the package sustained them.

By the time the plane made its bumpy touchdown late in the day, and they emerged in the middle of a dusty windstorm, they were both tired and stiff.

Danovitch got them through the terminal building and hailed a taxi. The driver barely allowed them time to settle themselves on the lumpy rear seat before he pulled away from the curb.

Dushanbe was a blend of ancient and modern. Its population contained a large percentage of Islamic Sunnites, and the influence of their culture and heritage showed in the city's architecture. Mosques shared space with modern buildings. The crowded streets were full of men and women in traditional costume, reminding Bolan that this part of Russia bordered on Afghanistan and China.

"I feel like a foreigner here myself," Danovitch said.

"I can see what you mean."

Bolan had been watching the driver, whose dark eyes kept studying them in the rearview mirror. The Executioner had a bad feeling about their driver.

They were dropped at the hotel that had been booked for them and went inside. The place was a far cry from the establishment Bolan had used in Moscow.

In his gloomy room, with its sparse furniture and rumbling, noisy plumbing, Bolan changed into fresh clothing. He strapped on his shoulder rig, checked the SIG-Sauer and holstered it.

He was about to leave when there was a tap at his door. It was Danovitch, changed and freshened up herself.

"Shall we go?" she asked.

On the street she hailed a passing taxi. Informing the driver of their destination, she turned to Bolan.

"I would be interested in knowing what this assignment is really about."

Bolan felt he should bring her up to date, but something deep inside warned him not to. He needed to be certain about her first. He'd been betrayed before by so-called allies. His nature forced him to be cautious, not because he had any hard evidence she was anything other than genuine, but more from an inbred instinct that forced him to be wary. If he wasn't, his reward could be a sudden and violent death.

"Let's see what we can turn up at Christophoulos's place first."

He saw her shoulders stiffen. She stared at him with her dark eyes.

"We are supposed to be partners, Mr. Belasko. This isn't how I see it. You don't trust me."

She remained silent for the remainder of the trip.

The taxi dropped them at the corner of a dusty street in the poorer section of town, the kind of place that attracted little attention from the police because it was probably dangerous to venture that far off the beaten track.

Danovitch became the professional police officer the moment they were out of the car.

"Christophoulos has an apartment on the second floor, the corner one overlooking the street."

She led the way, Bolan following. Before he entered the building, he noticed a taxi nosing around the corner at the other end of the street. He recognized the driver immediately. It was the same man who had brought them from the airport.

He headed for the stairs—Danovitch had already reached the first landing—and took the steps two at a time.

"Danovitch! Hold on!" he whispered.

His words went unheeded as she reached the second landing and turned to face the door to Christophoulos's apartment.

"Just ease off," Bolan said, coming up alongside her.

She reached out to check the door handle, which offered no resistance. She pushed the door open. The room inside was gloomy, with only a chink of light showing through a crack in the closed curtains.

Peering over the top of Danovitch's head, Bolan caught the merest sliver of light reflecting off metal—metal that turned in their direction.

It was all Bolan needed to realize they were walking into a setup.

9

Bolan shoved Danovitch hard between the shoulders, knocking her to her knees a split second before the bullets from a subgun pounded the wall plaster at head height. Powdery debris showered down filming the woman's dark hair with dust.

Bolan hauled the SIG-Sauer from its holster. He ducked below the stream of slugs as he entered the room, his eyes searching the shadows. The shooting ceased. His ears picked up a whisper of sound, and, peering in that direction, he caught the merest indication of movement. Then a faint glimmer of light again stroked the length of a gun barrel.

A large, wooden table loomed ahead of Bolan. Still crouching, he approached it, rounding the end and coming to rest on one knee. His eyes picked out some detail, gray and indistinct, but enough for him to identify the hunched form of a man cradling a subgun to his chest as he changed position.

Bolan settled the pistol on target and stroked the trigger. The weapon thundered in the confines of the room. He saw the hardman fall backward with a grunt of pain. A chair was overturned, and there was the sound of frantic scrabbling.

Bolan ran forward, flattening against the closest wall. Out the corner of his eye he saw that Danovitch was back on her feet, and closing in from the opposite side of the room.

Low mutterings from the far end of the room convinced Bolan the shooter wasn't alone. He heard the rattle of a weapon being lifted. He edged away from the wall and was rewarded by the sight of a man stepping out of the shadows, the subgun held ahead of him and aimed in the Russian cop's direction.

There was no time for a verbal warning.

Bolan triggered the P-226 twice, sending his warning in the form of 9 mm rounds that dropped the gunner in his tracks.

As the gunner fell, Bolan sensed movement closer at hand. He turned in time to see the second man emerge from the gloom, a large handgun in his big fist. The weapon spit a long gout of flame. The bullet clipped the top of Bolan's shoulder, causing him to draw a sharp intake of breath.

The gunner took a step forward, then his eyes opened wide with astonishment as his chest erupted into a bloody mess from the slugs coring into his back. He was spun out of control and slammed face-first into the wall, before slumping to the floor. The handgun slid across the carpet to stop at Bolan's feet.

Danovitch crossed the room, crouched by each man and checked them over.

"That's Christophoulos," Bolan said. "Do you know the other one?"

She rose to her feet.

"No. He was probably one of his hired thugs."

"Somebody is anxious for us not to get close to what's going on. We shouldn't hang around here too long."

Danovitch crossed the room to the telephone. "Let me just make a quick call. We have a few moments." When she was connected she spoke rapidly in Russian. Bolan was only able to pick up a few words and phrases, but he heard her mention Seminov's name. He guessed she'd gone directly to her superior. When she had completed her call, she turned to Bolan.

"I owe you my life," she said. "Thank you."

Her dark eyes searched his face.

"You are a strange person, but not a fool or a coward. I respect that."

"Respect is usually hard won, so I'd say we were even," Bolan said.

He decided it was time to bring her fully into the picture and she listened without interruption.

"This is terrible," she said finally. "If they succeed, who knows where they might explode this bomb?"

"Which is why we have to keep this to ourselves. If word leaks out that there's a nuclear bomb, we could end up with mass panic."

"Perhaps that's what these people want," Danovitch suggested. "To create unrest and fear. Or it could be some kind of massive blackmail scheme. Pay us what we want or your city will be bombed."

"It's possible," Bolan agreed.

"But you don't believe it's that simple?"

The soldier shook his head. "I have a feeling these people want more. This is too complicated a scheme just to end up with a truck full of money."

"Maybe it's political. Dissidents or terrorists. A power struggle within some large criminal organization."

She banged her fist against the wall.

"We're just standing and suggesting possibilities, but we're still no closer to any answers."

"Maybe we are," Bolan said.

"What do you mean?"

"The two men here. They both worked for Petrochenko?"

"Yes."

"What's our friend Petrochenko up to his neck in?"

"Everything and anything, buying and selling, as long as his services go to the highest bidder. He has contacts all over the world."

"We have photographic proof of Petrochenko in France, and his man Sheppard. They were meeting with Dr. Ralph Semple, an American who knows how to construct a nuclear device.

"When I showed up in Scotland to look into what Sheppard was doing there, the guy Sheppard was dealing with was killed off. Sheppard then set up a fake smuggling operation, and while everyone was chasing after that, he skipped the country, taking the item with him. An item we're pretty certain is the casing for a crude uranium-based nuclear bomb. I follow linking up with you. We pool our knowledge and pick up on Petrochenko. Information leads us here to Dushanbe. The minute we try to latch on to Christophoulos, we walk into a setup. What we need to know is where Sheppard is. I think he's more important than Petrochenko."

"Why?"

"You said yourself that Petrochenko is a dealer. He handles the money end, makes the promises. I'm pretty sure it's Sheppard who calls the shots on this deal. And his old stomping grounds are the mountains bordering Afghanistan."

"They are big mountains, Mr. Belasko."

"We need help to find him then."

"Go on."

"Sheppard's CIA days would have provided him with contacts. He'd know bases in the mountains on both sides of the border."

"The mountains are a good place to hide yourself and your activities."

"Talking about hiding, it might be worth checking this place over," Bolan said.

They started to search the room. Whatever else he might have been, Christophoulos hadn't been tidy or overly concerned about security.

In a drawer Bolan found a pair of handguns and loaded magazines. There was also extra ammunition. At the back of the same drawer he found a couple of small plastic bags containing low-grade cocaine.

"This guy either figured he was untouchable or he had good insurance," Bolan remarked.

"Do you mean he bought off the local police?"

"He must have felt pretty secure to leave stuff like this lying around."

They quickly went through the rest of the apartment. It yielded all kinds of contraband goods, plus more weapons and cocaine. There was also a great deal of money, stuffed in drawers and stored in boxes on shelves in the closets.

"Look at these," Danovitch said, dumping a number of videotapes on the table. Bolan picked up one and examined the label, but found he was unable to translate the Russian.

"They are pornographic movies," she explained. "This isn't what we abandoned communism for. It was to make Russia a better place for us all. Now we have more crime than ever before."

"It's the price of freedom," Bolan said. "Freedom brings out the bad as well as the good. There has to be a transition period, a fight to determine the will of the people. The good will come. Every society has criminals, whatever the political system. You just have to keep on fighting them. Never let them have one day when they're allowed to think they might be winning."

"Are you such a man, Mr. Belasko?"

"I do what I can," Bolan replied.

The telephone rang, the clamor loud in the apartment. Bolan gestured to Danovitch.

"Answer it," he said. "See if you can learn anything."

She picked up the phone, listened for a moment, then replied in Russian, her voice becoming low and husky.

The conversation went on for a couple of minutes, then she replaced the receiver.

"I convinced him that I was one of Christophoulos's lady friends. He had a reputation as a womanizer. The man needed to contact Christophoulos urgently. I told him he was staying out of sight because he was being investigated. The man was cautious but insisted he had to get information to Christophoulos. I arranged to meet him tonight near the train yard to act as a go-between."

"It could be risky. We can't be sure he trusts you fully. It might simply be a trap."

"Then I will have to rely on you to keep me out of trouble," the Russian said. "What other choice do we have? Time is short and we don't have too much to go on. If there's a possibility we can get closer to Sheppard and his group, then the risk is worth taking."

Bolan was forced to agree with her reasoning. He wasn't sure he liked the scenario, but as Danovitch had said they had little else to go on.

He went to the window overlooking the street. The taxi he'd spotted as he'd entered the building was gone. Bolan still had a bad feeling about the man and was certain he'd show up again.

Danovitch touched his arm.

"Your shoulder. Were you hit?"

"It was just a scratch. I'll survive."

"Let's get out of here so I can see to it for you." She flashed her eyes at him. "Do not argue with me."

"I wasn't about to," Bolan said—and meant it.

10

They reached the train yard just before darkness fell. A wind blew between the buildings as they crossed the street adjacent to the tracks. Only a few people were in the area.

"There's a café," Danovitch said. "We can wait there until it's time for the meeting."

"This still doesn't feel right," Bolan told her.

They sat down and the captain ordered coffee for them.

"I shouldn't criticize you," she said. "I trust few people myself. I'm not sure I even trust you, Mr. Belasko."

"Call me Mike. And I thought we'd left that behind."

She smiled. "Not trusting you doesn't mean I don't like you, or respect you."

"That's a start," Bolan admitted.

"You haven't told me what Seminov said when you called him."

"He asked if you were all right. I said you were and that we were following up on new information. He said also that he would speak to the commandant of the local police here in Dushanbe and arrange for the bodies to be taken care of."

Their coffee came. It was Turkish—very strong and hot.

They sipped at the brew, enjoying the moment of calm.

Bolan glanced at his watch. "It's time for us to go."

Danovitch paused at the door. "We follow the plan we discussed?"

Bolan nodded. "Try to stay where I can see you. I don't want you vanishing and something happening before I can reach you. This guy might not come alone."

Bolan watched her go. Then he crossed the street, sticking to the shadows of the buildings, and began to trail her. She was walking steadily, not rushing, and he was able to keep her in sight without getting too close.

As they reached a narrow street flanked by darkened buildings, Bolan became aware of footsteps behind him. It seemed he was about to be proved right. The contact hadn't come on his own.

Bolan checked on Danovitch. She was still in sight.

He spotted the mouth of an alley coming up. He dodged into it and flattened himself against the wall.

His tail showed in the mouth of the alley, peering into the gloom. Bolan caught a glimpse of something bulky in the man's hand as he moved. It was a gun. The tail eased into the alley. Bolan could hear the rustle of his clothing, the sound of his breathing. The odor of cheap after-shave reached him, the smell becoming stronger as the man got closer.

Bolan moved fast, a striking shadow coming out of the darkness. His left hand swept down in a hard chop that caught the tail's gun hand, numbing it. The weapon slipped from his nerveless fingers. Bolan kicked it aside, turning at the same time to catch hold of his adversary's coat, pulling him forward and around. He jabbed the outer edge of his right hand across the bridge of the man's nose. Something snapped with a soft sound and blood began to spurt from his nostrils, spilling down onto the front of his leather coat. He began to gag on the blood that ran down his throat. Bolan slammed him against the wall and unleathered the SIG-Sauer. He pressed the muzzle into the tail's cheek.

"Easy, pal!" the man protested. "Jesus, you broke my damn nose."

The accent was unmistakably American.

Bolan wasn't overly surprised. Sheppard was American. There was no reason why he shouldn't have brought in people of his own to strengthen his command of the operation. Borders were melting anyway, even vanishing altogether. Crime was crime, be it in Moscow or Chicago.

"Sheppard must be running out of options if he's hiring third-raters like you," Bolan said, flipping the man around to face the wall so he could frisk him.

"You won't be crowing when Sheppard gets his hands on you."

"In your position I wouldn't be so free with my mouth."

"Yeah? The hell with you, pal, and that lady cop! She's got a surprise coming when she sees who's waiting to meet her."

Alarm bells rang in Bolan's head. Danovitch *was* walking into a trap. His instincts had been right all along.

His captive, realizing he had said too much, made a sudden desperate lunge that got him away from the wall and Bolan's grip. He groped under his pants leg and came up with a short stabbing blade that he slashed up and around, catching Bolan's forearm. The keen edge cut through the soldier's jacket and shirt, slicing a hot line over his flesh. He pulled back, then arched forward, using the muzzle of his pistol to smash his opponent across the bridge of his broken nose. The man yelled, the pain forcing him to pause. That was his final mistake.

Bolan's left hand, palm uppermost, came around in a devastating arc that connected with the man's right temple, the blow shattering the fragile bone and driving it into his brain. The American was dead before he hit the ground.

Turning away, Bolan went after Danovitch. His confrontation had taken long enough for her to be lost in the darkness ahead.

He skirted the edge of the deserted buildings, ears straining to pick out any sound that might give him direction.

He moved on, filtering out the sounds of the train yard, the hiss of steam from a locomotive, the rattle of freight cars as they were shunted along a track.

Off to the left, he picked out the scrape of footsteps on loose gravel. He followed the sound, peering into the shadows, trying to separate movement from the static chunks of darkness.

Then came the low murmur of voices, one deeply male, the other Danovitch's, beginning to rise. There was laughter from two men.

Bolan felt a sense of urgency, the need for him to locate his targets and close in fast.

Danovitch yelled, loud enough for Bolan to get a lock on her position.

He raced forward, the SIG-Sauer already on track, homing in.

He rounded the corner of a shed. In the dull glow of an exterior wall light stood two men crowding Danovitch who had her back to the wall, facing her adversaries with defiance.

Bolan recognized one of the men from the photographs he'd seen: Vasily Petrochenko.

The other man was the taxi driver Bolan had been having bad feelings about.

Petrochenko held a large pistol in his left hand, the muzzle aimed at Danovitch. He said something to her, and Bolan saw her shake her head.

The big Russian lined up the muzzle of his pistol with Danovitch's head.

The taxi driver stepped back a pace or two.

That movement told Bolan that Petrochenko was about to fire.

The Executioner pushed away from the shed, the P-226 already centered on the gunner.

He didn't hesitate. His finger stroked the trigger, again and again. The slugs caught the big man between the shoulders. They punched him forward, the pistol in his hand flipping skyward. He cannoned into Danovitch crushing her against the wall as he fell. She threw out her hands to push him aside, her face spotted with his blood.

The taxi driver began to turn, hauling an equally large pistol from under his coat.

Bolan shot him on the move, firing several shots that cored into his arm and shoulder, spinning him all the way around. He slipped to his knees, still fisting his gun, and the Executioner tagged again. This time the round shattered the man's skull, bursting it open like an overripe melon.

The soldier reached Danovitch. Her eyes were wide with shock. She took a deep calming breath and wiped the spots of blood from her face.

"Petrochenko knew we were coming," she said. "There is a man named Gruyshin at the Ministry of Security in Moscow. Apparently he's been working for Petrochenko for months, keeping him up to date with police movements. He'd been selling out our officers for money and a cut in one of the dope trafficking rings in Moscow."

"He knew we were working together?"

"Yes. Now I can understand why my unit has been blocked every time we went for something. Gruyshin has been watching us all the time, sending information back to Petrochenko. The taxi driver was a local agent in his employ, too." Her tone changed. "How can we defeat these people when they buy into the units supposed to be fighting them? Who can we trust?"

"You said yourself you don't trust easily. You have to stay that way if you want to survive. In most cases you work on instinct, make your own judgments."

She sighed and leaned against the wall.

"So, where do we go from here?"

"First you'd better call Seminov and let him know about Gruyshin."

Danovitch crouched beside the taxi driver and went through his pockets. She pulled out various items, studying them, then examined his clothing.

"He isn't from Dushanbe originally. These clothes are homemade. They look like the sort from the mountain region to the south. Here, look at this."

She showed Bolan an ID card bearing the taxi driver's photograph.

"He's from a village in the southern Pamirs. That's close to the mountain route that eventually leads into Afghanistan. This man would guide Petrochenko's people in and out of the mountains."

"Then that's where we're heading," Bolan said. "I think we're on the right track."

11

Slopes of the Pamir Mountain Range

The landscape had changed dramatically. The sky dominated the craggy ramparts of the Pamir Mountains. The air was thinner, drier, carrying a smell of dust that drifted on the breeze. Beyond the serrated crags lay Afghanistan.

Bolan and Danovitch had made the journey from Dushanbe by bus—an ancient vehicle that had wound its way from the city across the dry terrain.

Wearing rough peasant clothing, their weapons hidden beneath the folds, Bolan and Danovitch were posing as a pair of itinerant workers seeking employment. The bus driver didn't think they stood much of a chance. Their destination, the home village of Vaska, the dead taxi driver, was a poor place, struggling to raise crops in the harsh climate. There was some livestock around, too, but he didn't think anyone would be taking on helpers.

As the bus wound its way along the rough, single track road, Danovitch glanced over at Bolan. They were seated at the rear of the bus, away from the other few passengers.

"We did agree this was the best way to get closer. If we walked in dressed the way we were, we wouldn't get the time of day," she said.

"Let's hope we guessed right, then."

"Do you have doubts?"

"Nothing is ever as cut and dried as it seems."

"The village is at the start of the trail that leads through the mountains into Afghanistan. It would be an advantageous spot for Sheppard and his people. It's a remote area with little official administration. The government already has enough to deal with in the main areas of the country. Smuggling and dealing in contraband has been a tradition in these areas for as long as anyone can remember."

"Not the kind we're dealing with."

"I agree, but look at those mountains. Once in there it would be very easy to hide anything."

Bolan accepted the logic of her argument. Mason Sheppard and his partner, Petrochenko, did their illicit dealing in an area where demand and supply were never still. Sheppard's speciality was weapons. He had the knowledge and contacts to push his merchandise all around the area: Afghanistan, Pakistan, Iraq and Iran. All those countries were in unsettled states, and the need for weapons seldom waned. It was a billion-dollar industry, ripe and ready for exploitation by a man with Sheppard's talents.

His CIA experience had given him the knowledge, paid him to nurture contacts, and Sheppard had done that well. He was well equipped to fulfill the needs of his clients. Morality and loyalty didn't feature in the equation—he did it for the money and nothing else.

Now it seemed he was moving up a notch, from conventional arms to the ultimate weapon of destruction.

THE BUS DROPPED THEM on the outskirts of the village. Bolan slung his bag over his shoulder and pulled the cloth cap he wore down his forehead.

They made their way up the sloping, dusty road into the village. The locals watched their approach, but no one challenged them.

They crossed the tiny central square to a low building with a timbered roof. The interior was hazy with smoke from a crude cooking stove holding blackened pots. A long table occupied the middle of the room, with benches running down its length. Only three people sat at the table. They glanced up as Bolan and Danovitch entered, then returned to their food.

Earlier, Bolan had suggested that she do all the talking for them. His Russian was good enough to get by on a basic level, but not strong enough for rapid conversation. He would play dumb, allowing her to carry them through.

Bolan sat at the table, while Danovitch went to the far end and ordered them plates of the stew that appeared to be the only thing on offer. Bolan saw her point to him, then point to her mouth.

She brought the food to the table. Bolan didn't have to act the part of a hungry man. Their journey had been long, and they hadn't had much time for food.

The other three diners finished their meal and left. Danovitch leaned close to Bolan and spoke softly.

"I asked if we might get work, told the man we were willing to do anything. He said there was nothing here for us. When I said we'd been told to come here by Vaska, he went very quiet."

"If that doesn't get a reaction, nothing will," Bolan said.

They finished their meal and wandered outside to sit on a bench.

Some time later a battered old truck appeared and parked across the square. One of the two men in the cab climbed out and went around to the rear of the eating house. He was inside for no more than a couple of minutes. When he returned he went directly to the truck and spoke to the man behind the wheel. More than once the two men turned to look toward Bolan and Danovitch.

"I think we've been tagged," Bolan muttered.

"What do we do?"

"Stand up and walk. Don't rush. Just like we were moving out of the village."

They stood, making a play about picking up their bags, Danovitch guiding Bolan as if he were a little slow. They moved across the dusty square and took the single road out of the village. They had just cleared the last house when they heard the growl of the truck's engine and knew it was following them.

The road they were on was single track, heading toward the higher slopes of the mountains. Bolan let Danovitch walk ahead, his right hand inside his coat, fingers around the butt of the SIG-Sauer.

The truck lurched into view. It moved slowly, belching smoke from its exhaust. The driver brought it to within a few feet of Bolan.

Danovitch turned and grabbed his arm, pushing him to the side of the road. The truck driver leaned out his window and yelled at them. A few feet on, he stepped on the brakes and brought the truck to a halt.

The cab doors opened and the driver and passenger climbed out. They were both armed, the butts of their SIG-Sauer P-226 pistols sticking out from their belts.

The driver spoke heavily accented English.

"It's a pity that you are going to die when you are so close!"

Bolan simply stared at him, playing the role of mute, pretending not to understand.

The driver returned his stare. Bolan guessed he was going to force the issue.

What he didn't anticipate, or expect, was the driver's means of precipitating a response.

Still facing Bolan, the driver snatched the SIG-Sauer from his belt, raised the muzzle, then turned slightly and shot Danovitch.

12

The sound of the shot echoed around them. The ejected cartridge case struck the ground, and there was a gasp of pain from Danovitch as she was spun off her feet.

Bolan had no time to draw the P-226.

He stepped up to the driver as the man began to turn his way again. He grabbed the driver's gun arm, his big hand closing over the man's finger, inside the SIG's trigger guard. Without pause, Bolan pushed the driver's hand in the direction of his partner and pulled the trigger of the pistol as the muzzle acquired its target. The 9 mm slug cored into the man's skull, blowing out the back in a bloody fountain. With his hand still clamped over the butt of his own gun the man crashed to the ground.

Still keeping his grip on the driver's gun hand, the Executioner rammed his elbow into his midsection. The man grunted as he sagged to his knees. Bolan twisted the man's gun arm, putting pressure on the elbow joint and holding it there. Ignoring the driver's howl of pain, he drove the heel of his left palm into the man's jaw, putting every ounce of strength into the blow. It snapped the driver's teeth together with splintering force and broke his jaw in three places. The driver was slammed up against the side of the truck. Bolan followed, taking hold of the SIG-Sauer by the barrel and yanking it from the man's hand.

But the driver wasn't done yet. He reached in behind his belt and dragged out a slim-bladed knife. He pushed himself away from the side of the truck and launched himself at Bolan.

A shot rang out.

The driver's face dissolved into crimson as the bullet cored into the side of his nose. He slewed to the left and fell against the truck's fender.

Bolan turned in the direction of the shot. Danovitch lay propped up on her left arm, her pistol in her right hand.

"How would you survive without me, Mike?"

It was the last thing she said before she passed out.

Bolan knelt beside her, checking her wound. The bullet had entered her left shoulder close to the armpit, passing through her flesh to emerge at the rear. He knew the bleeding had to be stopped quickly. He propped her up against a rock, then peeled away her upper clothing until he had the wound exposed. He found a canteen of water in the cab of the truck and soaked a wad of cloth he formed from her spare shirt. He washed the wound, then made thick pressure pads from more material and bound them in place. He then restored her clothing.

Turning his attention to the dead men, Bolan relieved them of their weapons and spare ammunition. Opening the rear of the truck, he placed the bodies inside, covering them with a canvas sheet. He put his and Danovitch's bags in the space behind the seats in the cab. Picking up the still unconscious woman, he settled her in the passenger seat, then took his place behind the wheel and started the engine. He dropped the truck into gear and moved off along the dusty trail, pushing deeper into the mountainous terrain.

Danovitch opened her eyes about an hour later. When she moved, the pain from her shoulder drew a soft groan from her lips.

"Try not to move too much," Bolan advised.

"That's difficult to do with the way you drive," she grumbled.

Bolan couldn't help smiling. "You must be recovering," he said.

"Where are we?"

"Up-country. This looked to be the only way into the mountains, so I took it. Since then, there hasn't been a turnoff, so I'm assuming we're still on the right road."

"It'll be dark soon," she said.

"We'll rest until morning. I also need to check that wound of yours."

Danovitch made a cursory inspection of her bandaged shoulder. "How did you manage to do this while I was unconscious?"

"The best I could."

Darkness swept across the mountains quickly. The temperature began to drop, as well. Bolan pushed on a little farther, then pulled the truck to the side of the track and cut the engine.

Before it became too dark, he checked her wound, replacing the pressure pads with fresh ones. He was aware of her close scrutiny as he tended her injury, the feel of her flesh.

"I have much to thank you for, Mike," she said, drawing her shirt back across her shoulder.

"It needed doing," Bolan said. "Besides, I need to thank you, too."

Danovitch smiled slightly. She was realizing that this Mike Belasko was more than just a man of action. There was much she would've liked to learn about him, but in their present situation survival against the odds took precedence. Soul searching would have to come later.

There was no food in the truck, only the water canteen. They each had a drink.

"You rest," Bolan told her. "I'll keep watch. As soon as it's light we'll go on."

She settled down inside the truck cab, closing the windows to keep out the night chill. Bolan wrapped himself in his rough clothing, set himself close to the truck and prepared to wait out the night.

He had taken the SIG-Sauer automatics, checked that they were loaded and had a shell in the chamber. He placed one on top of the front truck wheel close to where he sat. The other he kept in the large coat pocket. His own P-226 was still in place behind his belt.

Bolan listened to the night sounds, as the hours passed.

SOMETIME LATER, he raised himself, stretching to ease the kinks from his body. He stuck his hands deep in the pockets of his coat and took a slow turn around the truck.

He was on his return when something made him stop. He turned his head, listening.

At first he thought he'd imagined it, but then the sound came again.

He'd been right the first time. Something—or someone—was out there.

Bolan peered into the darkness beyond the truck. His eyes were well adjusted to the night, so he was able to pick out the shapes moving from rock to rock. He took the P-226 from the pocket of his coat.

Easing back to the side of the truck, he unlatched the cab door.

"Tanya," he whispered urgently, "wake up."

"I am awake. What is it?"

"Visitors."

"Sheppard's people?"

"Most likely."

Danovitch took her pistol from inside her coat.

"You stay in here. Keep down," Bolan said.

She nodded. As he made to close the door, she reached out to touch his cheek.

"Be careful."

Bolan pressed the door shut. He crouched and headed to the front of the truck, using the big wheel as cover. He scanned the surrounding terrain, ears tuned to the slightest sound. After a few seconds he picked up the soft movements of the approaching group. He was able to pinpoint at least four of them. He knew that there could be others, coming in on the far side of the truck, and maybe more at the rear. He would have to deal with them on a visual basis.

Another minute passed with agonizing slowness.

A sudden noise shattered the silence. Someone had stepped on a loose stone. Bolan, searching the source of the sound, saw a dark shape looming. Thin moonlight glanced off the metal of a gun barrel.

"To hell with this!" came a strained whisper. "Let's hit them now!"

Bolan tracked the voice with his pistol, then fired. The slug found its mark, tossing the target off his feet. The stricken man cried out, then his voice trailed off.

The Executioner ducked under the high chassis of the truck, dropping flat on the ground.

His adversaries came forward in a ragged line. There were three of them, their weapons held in front of them.

Bracing the SIG-Sauer in both hands, Bolan snapped off a volley of shots, moving back and forth with the muzzle.

One man went down, spewing blood from his lacerated throat. The other two opened fire, stitching the truck with autofire. Bolan used the muzzle-flashes as target indicators. His next volley took out the second attacker. The third man had almost reached the truck before the Executioner cored his left knee with a tri-burst. The man went down screaming in agony, his subgun discarded as he clutched both hands to his shattered knee, blood spurting between his fingers.

Rolling over, Bolan cleared the chassis. He pushed to one knee, the P-226 sweeping back and forth. He picked up an onrushing figure and drilled a pair of slugs into him.

He sensed someone close behind him and whirled, arcing the handgun around. Something hard struck his right shoulder, slowing him. As he turned to meet his attacker, he felt a blow across the side of his head. It drove him back against the side of the truck. Blood began to run down the side of his face.

In the background Bolan heard Danovitch yell in fury. Her cry spurred him on and he fielded the next blow, delivering a solid elbow smash that drew a grunt of agony from the target.

The sudden rattle of gunfire blocked out any other sounds. Bolan heard glass shatter, felt the truck rock as a sustained burst of fire raked the cab.

"Tanya!" he yelled.

Close by someone expelled a gush of air as he exerted himself. Bolan's head exploded as the blow landed, and he dropped to his knees.

The SIG-Sauer was snatched from his hand. Other hands pulled at his clothing, frisked him expertly and removed the reserve P-226.

"Up on your feet, you bastard!"

The order was emphasized by a vicious kick that connected with Bolan's ribs.

With a gunner on either side of him, he was dragged around to the far side of the truck where others were waiting. The sound of an engine heralded the arrival of a Jeep. It came to a stop on the fringe of the area, its headlights illuminating two dead men on the ground and the one who lay nursing his shattered knee.

"Damn son of a bitch!" someone yelled at the sight.

Bolan saw someone lunge at him. He tried to pull aside, but a gun butt cracked against the side of his head.

"We should kill the mother now!"

"We can't kill him. Shut up and let's get a grip."

His head on fire, Bolan waited and listened.

A voice called out in Russian.

"What'd he say?"

Someone laughed. "He says the bitch is dead!"

Bolan's world shrank to a small, white-hot cell. He only had himself to think of now.

He forced himself to look as they pulled Danovitch's body from the bullet-riddled cab. His silent rage was fueled by the callous way they dragged her out of the door and down the metal step. They dropped her on the ground once she was clear. A booted foot turned her over.

There was a hurried conversation between one of the Russians and the American who appeared to be the head man. Finally satisfied, the American nodded to his companions.

"It's her," he said. "The cop from the OCD."

"The one Sheppard told us about?"

"Yeah. Teamed up with this hotshot."

He turned to look at Bolan.

"What do you think of your buddy now?"

Bolan remained silent. His thoughts about Tanya Danovitch right then were personal. He would save his reaction for later.

There was an angry yell from the rear of the truck. The bodies under the canvas sheet had been discovered. Two of the Russians began to argue violently. One leapt down from the truck and hurled himself at Bolan, swinging the butt of his Kalashnikov at the Executioner's head. Bolan ducked and the rifle met empty air. The Russian reversed the assault rifle, his finger seeking the trigger. It was only the efforts of the others that kept him from shooting Bolan there and then.

"Let me tell you something," one of the Russians said. "You're living on borrowed time."

"Let's get the hell out of here," the American shouted. He turned to Bolan. "Over to the Jeep, pal, and don't try any clever tricks. Sheppard needs you alive at least until he has a talk with you. After that I don't figure you'll get much time to yourself."

As Bolan trailed after the American, aware that a number of guns were trained on him, the Russian who had lost control gave vent to his feelings by slamming the butt of his rifle into Bolan's back. The Executioner exaggerated the impact and fell against the truck. He used the opportunity to slump against the front wheel, and in the precious seconds before he was hauled upright, he closed a hand over the SIG-Sauer he had planted there earlier. He struggled upright, clutching his body in pretended pain, and shoved the P-226 into the waistband of his trousers, beneath his coat.

Bolan was shoved into the back of the Jeep. He saw that a couple of the men had stayed behind to retrieve the bodies of their companions and load them into the back of the truck. The Jeep moved off, back the way it had come, headlights burning twin tunnels in the darkness.

The truck caught up with them twenty minutes later. Bolan wondered if they'd placed Danovitch's body in the rear of the vehicle along with the dead men.

They traveled for more than four hours, climbing all the time. The way had become harsher, the mountain peaks looming over them. The night had turned colder and Bolan huddled into his coat, allowing himself to draw comfort from the feel of the P-226 nestled against his side.

In the hours ahead, the weapon might prove to be his only chance to stay alive in a situation that was closing in on him with startling rapidity.

13

The Jeep slowed and made a sharp turn. Bolan looked around and saw that the darkness was receding, giving way to a gray dawn.

Ahead, Bolan saw a stone-colored fortress perched on the edge of a plateau. It looked out across the crags, giving an unrestricted view over miles of mountainous terrain.

One of the Americans spoke. "Over there is Afghanistan. The place up ahead used to be some kind of Russkie outpost against the ravaging hordes. It was abandoned for a lot of years, until it got itself resurrected and dragged into the new Russia as part of free enterprise."

The man chuckled at his own joke. He was tall and lean. Thick blond hair showed under the well-worn baseball cap he wore. His eyes studied Bolan closely.

"I can see your damn mind at work, trying to figure if you can snatch my gun and shoot us all to hell before we get you. Don't try it. All it'll get is you dead and me having my throat torn out by Sheppard. Anyway, there isn't a damn place to hide here. Not unless you know the country."

Bolan knew he was going to have to play it carefully. If he acted too subservient they would get suspicious, while some kind of aggressive move would undoubtedly get him hurt. For now he was going to have to do it their way.

The Jeep, followed by the truck, rolled through a set of gates. Bolan unobtrusively checked the layout of the place as they crossed the courtyard that fronted the main building.

"Let's go," the American guard said.

Bolan was herded into a large, open room that contained little furniture, but held a considerable amount of computer equipment. Screens were up and running, and printers clattered noisily, spilling paper into baskets set behind them.

Bolan recognized Mason Sheppard before he'd fully turned around from his computer. The last time he'd seen Sheppard had been in Scotland, leading Andrew Greigson on a walk that proved to be his last.

Sheppard examined Bolan.

"Do you know what you've cost me?"

"Quite a lot," Bolan replied. "I hope it's set your schedule back."

"I'll tell you something, Belasko, or whoever you really are. You've upset the tight scheduling, but we

can make that up. There's no way you're about to
prevent this from going ahead.''

Bolan wished he knew exactly what Sheppard was
involved in. He needed to know the nuclear device's
destination, or get an opportunity to find and destroy the device.

The American stepped forward and placed the
confiscated weapons on the table.

"A bunch of our guys are dead," he said, "but we
took out the Russian cop."

"The price is getting higher all the time, Sheppard," Bolan said. "Maybe you want to recon-
sider."

Sheppard shook his head. "Every business has
setbacks, Belasko. You allow for them."

"You expect to stay untouched up here forever? It
won't happen. Too many people are involved now."

Sheppard glanced around, exaggerating his ex-
amination of the room.

"All I see is one man. Where's your backup, Belasko? Somehow I don't see the Marines coming
down the pass to cut us off. Mister, you are on your
own. We both know it. You caused me some problems back in Scotland, but in a way you did me a favor. While you were checking out McClain and
making noise, I was already off the coast in a light
plane, flying low under the radar all the way to Stavanger. By the time the coast guard pulled in Mc-

Clain's boat and found he was carrying a crate full of scrap metal, I was already on my way here."

"With Petrochenko providing the means."

"Yeah, he made things easy over here. The guy has clout. He knows who to buy off, who to avoid. It's easier now since they kicked out the hard-liners. The trouble is, the price just went up. It's the first thing democracy teaches—hike up the price. If the people want it, make them pay."

"Who's paying for your special package, Sheppard?" Bolan asked.

Sheppard paused, a slow smile curling his lips.

"That's bugging you, Belasko, isn't it? Your cause is lost, but you still need to know."

Sheppard glanced at the man behind Bolan.

"You reckon we should enlighten him, Phil? Figure it's safe?"

Phil shrugged. "It's on its way. There's not much he'll be able to do about it when he's dead."

"I'll think about it," Sheppard said. "One way or another, Belasko, you're a dead man. By the way, I take it Petrochenko's dead? If he'd handled the situation in Dushanbe, you wouldn't have got this far. Likewise that idiot Christophoulos."

He gave up and began to head for the door.

"I'll show you around, Belasko. I think you'll be impressed by my setup here."

Bolan fell in just after Sheppard. Phil walked close behind Bolan, the muzzle of his assault rifle trained on the Executioner's spine.

Sheppard became chatty. "Best time of my life was with the CIA. When they put me in Afghanistan, it was like coming home. Got to know the people and the country. I hated leaving, but the situation changed and the new regime was starting to get scary. Not that I liked what I saw when I got home, either. The country was going to hell in a handcart. And the Company was the same. They were out of control themselves, with their double-dealing and dirty tricks. Worse than some of the scum we were supposed to be fighting. So I did some bitching. They said you don't like it, Sheppard, you get out. So I did. You know what? They tagged me as a loose cannon. Sent their termination squads to take me out. Hell, it was too damn easy. I sent them home in their own tote bags."

"And now you want to get your own back, is that it, Sheppard? Selling weapons to anyone who has the cash to buy. Then going the final step and taking on a contract to build a nuclear bomb for some crazy." Bolan shook his head. "Makes you no better than the one who has his hand on the button."

Sheppard rose to the bait, his eyes blazing with anger.

"Damn you, Belasko. I served my country well. I carried out every dirty assignment they gave me. I did a lot of things I wasn't proud of, but I was doing it for my country. I believed every damn lie they told me. I danced their tune until I had my eyes opened."

"So life went sour on you," Bolan said. "You trying to tell me you believe it never happened to anyone else? If we roll over and start whining, then we end up no better than the enemy."

"I looked a lot deeper than you did. Far as I can see the whole damn country has gone to the dogs. It's open house these days. Take the money and run. Doesn't matter who the paymaster is, and that's what I'm doing."

They reached the far side of the compound. Sheppard stopped in front of a set of high steel doors. He pressed a button set in the wall, and the doors rumbled open. He led the way into a storage facility built from stone, with strip lighting in the ceiling.

The area was stacked with packing cases and cartons. Bolan didn't need to go too close to guess what they contained: weapons of every description, from assault rifles and handguns, to light and heavy machine guns, metal boxes of ammunition, grenades, handheld rocket launchers.

"Business is good," Sheppard said, "and it's getting better all the time. It's tough filling all the orders. Petrochenko had strong contacts, and they keep the goods rolling in." He grinned suddenly. "You did me a favor actually, offing Petrochenko. I guess I'll have to run the whole thing myself now."

"So why do you need the nuclear device?" Bolan asked.

"Persistent, isn't he?" Sheppard said to Phil.

"Too damn nosy," Phil answered. He jabbed the muzzle of his weapon against Bolan's spine. "You should ask me, but you won't like the answer I give you."

"Easy, Phil. After all, the man's only doing his job. Look, Belasko, the device is a one-off for a client, just a piece of merchandise. He pays the price, and I don't ask what he wants to do with it. I don't give a damn."

"Would you feel that way if he detonated it in your hometown?"

Sheppard laughed. "You ever been to my hometown? He'd be doing me, and it, a favor. Don't feed me any of that crap, Belasko. Home, country and Mom's apple pie lost its appeal a long time ago."

They were interrupted by one of Sheppard's men.

"There's a call for you. It's Colonel Dupre—"

Sheppard silenced the man with a wave of his hand. He turned to Phil.

"Take Belasko somewhere he can't do any harm."

"Why don't I shoot him right now?"

"Because I don't choose to have him shot right now. I need to find out who sent him here. The more we know the better we'll be able to cover our tracks. Lock him up, then join me."

Sheppard strode across the compound, leaving Bolan alone with Phil.

"Let's move, Belasko, and never mind what Sheppard says. Give me any trouble, you're dead."

They crossed to the far side of the compound. Where Sheppard had gone up stone steps to the upper level, Bolan was led along a dimly lit, dank passage. He was pushed into a small, stone cell and a heavy door was slammed shut behind him.

The cell was bare except for a low trestle bed. A small barred window was set high in the wall. Bolan sat down and listened to the sound of receding footsteps.

Dupre.

The name meant something. He delved deep into his memory, repeating the name over and over.

Then it came—Colonel Jules Dupre, deposed leader of the Caribbean island of St. Maritan, a brutal dictator who had ruled his island's population with a reign of terror until the U.S., impatient with his lies and political double-dealing, had sent in a task force and removed the man. Dupre's security force, known as the Black Skulls, had put up a bloody resistance, killing anyone who got in their way. In the end, St. Maritan was free of its repressive regime, but Colonel Dupre and a squad of his security men had managed to flee the island.

It was found that Dupre had been systematically bleeding his country dry. Billions of dollars had been siphoned off, hidden in secret accounts across the world.

Dupre relocated himself, surrounded by his Black Skulls, on an island off the Colombian coast. He kept a low profile for six months, then began to issue warnings that he was returning to St. Maritan. America would regret that day it interfered in his country's affairs.

Perhaps Bolan had just learned the identity of the nuclear device's purchaser.

14

"I can assure you, Colonel, that everything is under control," Mason Sheppard said.

There was a lengthy silence from the other end of the line. Sheppard waited. He had learned early on that Colonel Jules Dupre used silence as a way of unnerving people. All it did now was annoy Sheppard, but he kept his feelings in check. There was no point in antagonizing the man, not in the middle of a deal liable to earn Sheppard a lot of money.

"My Intelligence people tell me that you have been experiencing some interference with your operation," Dupre said finally. His voice was low, refined almost. But the man was a cold-blooded killer. He had been known to personally execute his opponents, both military and political.

"That's over now," Sheppard said. "I have the operative who has been causing some minor problems. He'll be taken care of."

"I hope so," Dupre said. "Let's get down to business. Is the package in transit?"

"Yes. It left early yesterday."

"The moment my people take delivery, the rest of your money will be deposited."

"That's fine, Colonel. Should we set a date now to discuss your future needs?"

"I admire a man who looks to the future. Let us say two weeks from today. At the same location we last met."

"I look forward to it, Colonel. Good luck with your project."

"Luck has nothing to do with it, Mr. Sheppard. Planning and full utilization of available resources are what it's all about."

The line went dead. No goodbye. Dupre, as usual, made the best use of his words as well as his time.

Sheppard replaced the receiver. He lingered for a moment, thinking about Mike Belasko. He had intended to question the man about his involvement with the OCD, and how much information they had on himself and his late partner, Petrochenko. Sheppard realized that was a little too late. Obviously there had been enough intel to take Belasko and the woman all the way to Dushanbe, and from there to Vaska's village. The fact that they'd tangled with Christophoulos and Petrochenko, as well as Vaska, meant they were digging pretty deep into the fabric of the organization. That meant they were closer to

Sheppard than was comfortable. It might also mean that they had learned about Gruyshin. If that was true, then he stood to lose a good contact in Moscow.

Sheppard was no fool when it came to staying alive and ahead of the game. When the flame got too hot you closed the door and moved away from the source. He would leave this place with great reluctance. It had been good for him, but he had no intention of it becoming his tomb.

Sheppard yanked open the door and called out. The armed man who responded carried a Heckler & Koch MP-5, slung from his shoulder by its webbing strap.

"Pass the word," Sheppard said. "This place is closed for business. Load the trucks. I want to be out of here before dark. Jack, I want you to personally supervise collecting all the computer disks. Nothing is to be left behind that might link anyone to us. Burn all the paperwork, and blow the computer room when we leave."

Jack nodded. He didn't question Sheppard. It had been drilled into them that they carried out his orders and didn't ask why.

Sheppard turned and made his way downstairs. He spotted Phil and crossed to him.

"I just gave the order, Phil. We're moving out of here. Belasko found us, so might others. I'll call ahead and make final arrangements to get us to the next location."

"Do you have anything special for me?" Phil asked.

Sheppard smiled at the man's eagerness.

"Belasko? Okay, you win. Kill him. Now."

"About damn time," Phil said, unslinging his assault rifle.

He strode away, heading for the cell block.

BOLAN HEARD THE OUTER DOOR crash open, followed by the thump of footsteps on the hard stone.

He rolled off the cot and moved to the corner of the cell opposite the door. Tugging the SIG-Sauer loose, he held the weapon in front of him, two-handed.

He didn't know who was coming, or why. The odds were against him, but his instincts told him to go for the opening, no matter how tight it might turn out to be.

Someone pounded on the cell door.

"Time's up, Belasko."

Bolan heard bolts snap back. The heavy door was booted open, swinging inward on rusting hinges. A shadow fell across the cell floor, the shape of a man carrying an assault rifle.

"Don't mess with me Belasko. There's no back door."

The man cursed. Bolan recognized his voice. It was Phil.

"The hell with this!" Phil stepped into the cell, the muzzle of his rifle tracking back and forth. For a moment his face showed astonishment, then he picked up movement to his right. He wheeled, and saw Bolan with the gun.

The Executioner fired once, a single round that cored into Phil's skull and out the other side. The man swiveled, sagging back against the wall before crumpling to the stone floor.

Crouching, Bolan searched the corpse. He took two spare magazines for the Kalashnikov. There was also another P-226 holstered on Phil's hip. Bolan took that, quickly looping the belt around his own waist. He picked up the AK-74 and exited the cell. He reached the outer door and cracked it open, scanning the area.

The main gates, directly across from him, stood open. There was a great deal of activity going on. Two trucks backed up to the arms store and were being loaded.

Was Sheppard evacuating? If so, it meant Bolan would get no better chance to make his escape.

He spotted another truck, closer to him. Two men were bringing weapons out of one of the buildings and loading them in the rear of the truck.

Bolan waited until one of them had returned to the building, leaving his partner to hoist boxes over the tailgate, before slipping from the door of the cell block. He hugged the wall as he moved to the truck, coming up behind the loader.

He reversed the Kalashnikov and slammed the butt against the base of the man's skull, driving him face-first into the metal tailgate. The man dropped to his knees, clutching his bleeding face and moaning.

A shadow fell across the ground. Bolan spun in time to see the downed man's partner stepping out of a door, a couple of ammo boxes in his hands. The man took in the scene instantly. He dropped the boxes and made a grab for the pistol on his belt. Taking a long step forward, Bolan drove the rifle's barrel into the guy's throat, the impact crushing his windpipe. He then swung his weapon, clubbing his opponent across the side of the head, dropping him to the ground.

Swiftly skirting the side of the truck, Bolan opened the driver's door and pulled himself into the cab. He dropped the rifle on the passenger seat, at the same time reaching for the ignition. The engine caught instantly. He shoved the clutch to the floor and dropped the truck into gear. He jammed his foot on the gas and swung the wheel as the truck lurched forward.

He was halfway across the compound before anyone realized there was something wrong. A warning shout rang out, and men began to converge on the truck, some raising weapons.

Bolan swung the wheel, swerving the truck from side to side. He felt a thump as one of the armed hardmen was caught by the truck's fender. Moments later the rear wheel struck something that rolled and yielded.

The sound of autofire reached Bolan's ears. He felt the slugs striking the metal sides of the truck, and thanked whomever had designed the vehicle's thick body.

Ahead, he saw someone trying to close the gates. He stepped hard on the gas and felt the truck surge forward. The man at the gates looked over his shoulder and saw the vehicle bearing down on him. He cleared the area with seconds to spare. Bolan took the truck through, scraping against one of the gates. He swung the wheel hard to the right as he hit the dirt track, and the vehicle picked up speed as he hit a downgrade, dust billowing in the air behind him.

There was no turning back. Whatever the outcome, Bolan was committed.

He concentrated on keeping the truck on the rough road. The rocky bank on one side fell away, to be replaced by a sheer drop. The track itself was narrow, not allowing Bolan much room for error either way. His knuckles showed white from his iron grip on the vibrating wheel. The truck, sturdy as it was, hadn't been designed for high-speed travel on such a surface.

The Executioner dismissed thoughts of safety, risking everything in a full-tilt run, hauling the truck around hairpin bends, almost losing it a couple of times when the wheels missed the edge of the track before slamming back on firm ground.

Slugs continued to bounce off the truck's metal body. Bolan gave it everything he had. There was little to choose from.

Certain death behind him. Unknown dangers ahead.

Then he saw the narrow wooden bridge spanning a deep gorge ahead, directly in his path, with no other route to take.

He didn't hesitate. He gripped the wheel and kept his foot to the floor, taking the truck directly toward the bridge.

15

An hour later Bolan lay on a ledge against the mountainside, flat on his stomach, checking back the way he'd come, when he saw the ragged group of armed men moving upslope in his direction.

He watched them spread out across the slopes, guiding one another with handheld transceivers. Farther back he saw sunlight glancing off the lens of binoculars.

He checked out the rugged slopes below him. He had just climbed them himself and knew they were treacherous, layered with loose shale and larger rocks. More than once during his ascent he had lost his footing, slipping back yards for every few feet gained. His pursuers were going to encounter the same difficulties.

Bolan decided he would make it even harder for them. Opening one of the loaded sacks he'd carried from the wrecked truck, he took out three grenades. He pulled the pin on the first one, let the spring flip off the handle and lobbed it downslope.

A man yelled as he recognized the grenade, his cry lost in the boom of the explosion. The blast loosened a section of rock, sending it cartwheeling down the slope, scattering everyone in its path.

Bolan repeated the procedure with the other two grenades, throwing them in opposite directions. When the smoke and dust cleared, he saw two men were down. One lay facedown, the back of his jacket bright with blood. The other was partly buried under tumbled rock.

The soldier edged off the ledge. He reached for the next handhold, pulling himself higher.

Rifles were raised immediately and triggered. The slugs fell short, chipping at the rock beneath him.

Breathing hard in the thin mountain air, Bolan dragged himself over a rocky ridge. He looked back down the slope to where his pursuers had once again taken up the chase.

He quickly dropped two more grenades on them, which exploded with lethal impact. He wedged the AK-74 in the crook of his arm, taking one last backward glance before making his next major climb.

He saw the glint of sunlight on a rifle barrel the instant before it fired. He dropped, heard the crack of the shot and felt the slug burn the top of his left shoulder. He hit the hard ground, pulling himself around, the Kalashnikov briefly catching against an outcropping. He hauled the weapon into firing position, finger on the trigger.

The gunner showed himself, believing he'd scored a fatal hit. He was outlined against the clear curve of the sky as he stared in Bolan's direction.

The Executioner waited for him to step forward, before triggering the assault rifle. The slam of his shot struck the gunner hard. It turned him halfway around, so that Bolan's second shot caught him between the shoulders and drove him facedown on the ground.

Pushing upright, Bolan moved on, leg muscles straining as he clambered across the next slope of rock.

Somehow his pursuers were finding a quicker way up. How they were managing this was answered shortly as his ears picked up the sound of rotors beating the air. Bolan glanced over his shoulder and saw the helicopter speeding in his direction.

The chopper flew over, circled, then came back at him.

Rotorwash almost lifted Bolan off the slope. He rolled on his back, pressing himself against the ground.

The chopper was close enough for him to see the pilot's face. The side hatch was open, and a two-man team knelt beside a swivel-mounted machine gun, lacing the ammo belt into the weapon.

Bolan pulled up the AK-74. He flipped the select lever to automatic and loosed a burst that caught the gunner's mate chest high, flinging him across the cabin in a tangle of arms and legs. Sweeping the muzzle the length of the helicopter, Bolan raked the transparent canopy with a sustained burst. The Plexiglas starred, gaps showing. Blood splashed the inside. The chopper suddenly dropped, veering away from the slope.

The soldier pulled a grenade from his sack and flung it in the direction of the chopper. It fell short, but the explosion sent out shock waves that rocked the craft. The pilot sent the machine into a headlong dive, pulling it up abruptly just before it reached the ground. It spun wildly before making a hard, clumsy landing.

Slugs continued to tear into the ground around Bolan. He pushed himself up the slope, needing to escape the erratic but still deadly bursts. There was also the possibility of the chopper returning, and he wanted to be in less open country by that time.

The thought crossed his mind that the chopper could easily have dropped a number of armed men higher up the slope. If that was the case, he could find himself caught between two forces—one coming from below, the other working its way down-slope from above.

Bolan crouched behind an outcrop and checked the upper slopes. He saw one armed man, then another some yards to the right. Off to the left, and higher up, he saw two more.

They were all well within range of the AK-74. He snapped in a fresh magazine, pushed the selector to single shot and settled down to wait. He gave the approaching gunners time to clear a jumble of rock. They hesitated on the edge of the open area, aware that once they set foot on it they had no cover for some distance.

Bolan caught them during their moment of indecision. He settled the assault rifle on the one farthest away from him and stroked the trigger, tracking his next target even as the first man went down. The second gunner had turned in the direction of the shot, and Bolan put a bullet through his head, directly between the eyes. The impact flipped him on his back, and he lay staring up at the sun. The remaining two broke apart, firing as they moved, putting down a curtain of fire that landed nowhere near Bolan. He dropped the third man before he could reach cover, then swiveled and triggered two shots at the vanishing figure of the surviving gunner, who took a desperate, headlong dive behind a jagged outcrop.

Bolan headed for the next ridge of rock. He reached it and took cover, turning to look back, and saw the man break from cover. The Executioner shouldered the Kalashnikov and triggered a single 5.45 mm slug that cored his adversary's head and dropped him in his tracks.

Pushing upright again, Bolan set off up the slope, intending to reach the highest point and cross it before the rear group could close in.

The altitude and the gradient of the slope made the way torturous. The muscles in Bolan's legs began to burn, and beneath his thick clothing he started to sweat.

Far behind him someone yelled. His pursuers had spotted him. He heard the angry hum of slugs striking the slope below him. His opponents were having difficulty compensating for the steep rise of the slope, their shots falling well short.

Bolan plunged forward and took up a position on the side of the mountain. Twisting over on his back, he saw his pursuers strung out across the base of the slope, well below him. He dragged the looped sacks from around his neck. Opening the one containing the extra AK-74 magazines, he removed the clips and distributed them among his pockets. Then he took out the last three grenades. One by one he removed the pins and tossed the bombs downslope. As the first one exploded, he turned and hauled himself hand-over-hand up the slope, finally rolling over the top of the ridge.

He lay facedown, his body aching, sweat rolling down his face, his fingers raw from clawing at the rocks. A sudden rush of air lifted dust out of the crevices and hurled it across the ridge.

He lifted his head as a pounding, throbbing beat assailed his senses.

The chopper was back, hovering only yards away, the rotors ripping the dust off the ground and swirling it about in choking clouds.

The machine dropped to earth, rocking on its skids. A man emerged from the dust, a raised autoweapon in his hands.

Bolan knew who it was even before Mason Sheppard was fully visible. He was shouting something. The soldier saw his lips move but couldn't pick out the words. The man's face was pale with dust, his eyes blazing with anger. He turned the muzzle of the weapon on Bolan and pulled the trigger.

The Executioner had already moved, rolling back over the edge of the ridge. He slithered on the loose surface, and he would have tumbled helplessly down the slope if he hadn't grabbed the edge of the outcropping with his left hand. He let go of the assault rifle and caught hold of the butt of one of the P-226s under his coat.

He heard Sheppard approach, dislodging shale as he came over the ridge, searching for Bolan. Instead, he found himself staring down into the black muzzle of the P-226. Bolan fired, triggering the pistol with unerring accuracy.

Sheppard's features dissolved into a bloody mask. He stumbled back from the ridge, hands to his face, blood seeping through his fingers. He made a strange gurgling sound, then toppled backward, his body spasming.

By the time Bolan regained his feet, Sheppard was dead.

He went across to the helicopter. It was empty. Sheppard himself had to have been flying it. It stood idling, the rotors still churning up a thick cloud of dust. The soldier opened the hatch and climbed into the pilot's seat. He took a few moments to check the controls, making sure that the cracked Plexiglas didn't hamper his vision.

Increasing the power, he worked the hand and foot controls, stabilizing the chopper as it began to lift. He veered away from the rocky ridges of the mountains, flying steadily.

He needed to find a place where he could safely contact Commander Seminov, then Hal Brognola. The Executioner had to move on to the next phase of his mission, unearth background on Colonel Jules

Dupre and make the connection between the exiled dictator and the nuclear device. That might require a covert visit to the man's island sanctuary.

Somehow, somewhere, he needed to dig out the information that would lead him to the rogue bomb—and before it was detonated.

16

Caribbean Sea, Off Cielo Island, Colombia

Mack Bolan, dressed in light pants and a dark blue shirt, ducked his head as he entered the cabin of the motor cruiser. He nodded to the tall, sandy-haired man at the wheel and joined the other occupant at the chart table.

Bob Lang glanced up from the chart he was studying and ran a tanned hand through his thick hair. He looked out through the cabin window, casting an experienced eye over the craft already moored at the jetties ringing Cielo Bay.

"Money attracts money," he murmured. From the outside, he looked every part the wealthy playboy who came to Cielo to laze in the sun and gamble. His expensive clothing and the cruiser were all part of his cover. Lang was in fact part of a DEA unit assigned to long-term observation and information gathering on the Colombian drug cartels. Along with his partner, Sol Benares, Lang made regular trips to the island off the Colombian coast. He had been working that beat for almost eight months, and had been able to pass some useful information back to Washington, but he was becoming impatient at not being able to make any tangible contribution to the war against the Colombian narcobarons. For the first time though, Lang felt he might have an opportunity to do something real.

That was because of the man he knew only as Mike Belasko. Orders had filtered down from Lang's Washington HQ that he was to assist, in whatever way needed, the man he would meet in Kingston, Jamaica. Belasko would join Lang and Benares for their next trip to Cielo. His visit wasn't connected with the drug trade, but was considered highly important. Any operational decisions he made weren't to be questioned, and if anything he did compromised Lang's covert presence, then the DEA was to take a back seat.

Lang hadn't been certain what to expect. Belasko had seemed to be a quiet, almost reserved man at first, but it wasn't long before the agent became aware of Belasko's presence. There was something about the man that brought out the best in Lang, gave him a sense of his own worth. It was obvious, too, that the man knew his way around, had knowledge of the business Lang was in. Belasko, the DEA man realized, had been there and knew the dark side of the human condition.

Placing his hands on the edge of the chart table, Bolan scanned the map Lang had laid out.

"This is where we're coming in?" he asked, his finger tracing a line.

"That's right. The place where Dupre hangs out is on the other side of the island. The estate overlooks the sea and has its own beach line. Dupre has the place under tight security. His own people, who came with him from St. Maritan, take care of that. They don't use any of the island people. Even the house staff is Dupre's. The man doesn't trust anyone except his own."

"I was examining his file last night," Bolan said. "The money he brought from St. Maritan, plus whatever the Colombians had been holding for him, make him a very rich man."

"What good is it doing him?" Sol Benares asked. "The guy can't leave the island. He's safe under Colombian law only as long as he stays on Cielo. If he goes into international waters, he'll be arrested. He's a walking dead man."

"Dupre wouldn't see it that way," Bolan said. "As far as he's concerned, the rest of the world betrayed him. His life is dedicated to regaining power on St. Maritan. The fact that he'll probably never achieve that doesn't enter his mind. He's sitting over there making his plans, arranging deals, bribing and coercing like he's always done. He feels he's been done a great injustice. All he wants is to make America pay for removing him from power."

"Then he's crazy," Benares replied. "He's a crazy walking dead man."

Lang smiled. "Puts his finger right on it. Wish I had that kind of insight."

"It takes a lifetime of practice," Benares quipped.

"The Colombians seem to have faith in him," Bolan said. "Why would they offer him sanctuary if he wasn't of any use to them?"

"Dupre had a good network going while he was president of St. Maritan. He was pushing coke all over the Caribbean, even into Miami. That network is still around. Word is Dupre's still pushing, not as much, but enough to keep the cartel happy."

"So he's still earning money for them?"

Lang nodded. "They let him have the estate free of charge. The cost is nothing when you make the kind of money they do."

Benares nosed the cruiser into one of the empty berths and cut the power as Lang went on deck to tie up the boat. As the motors fell silent, he glanced out the cabin window fronting the dock.

"Here comes the welcoming committee."

Bolan watched three uniformed men approaching. Lang had told him about the local cops. They checked passports and were happy to issue visas. There was little formality, except for the bribe that was expected. A refusal to pay up was frowned upon, and in some cases, protestors had been hauled off to the local jail until they saw sense.

Lang had prepared Bolan, and the Executioner's passport was ready and fully paid up.

The cops climbed on board and made their way into the cabin. The man in charge checked Bolan over with a practiced eye.

"First time to Cielo?" he asked.

Bolan nodded. "I heard the gambling was good and the nightlife interesting. I needed a break, so when my two friends here asked me along, I figured why not?"

"Passport?" the cop asked.

Bolan handed it over. The man opened it, and his eyes flickered over the hundred-dollar bills tucked inside. He turned his back to his colleagues, removed the cash and slipped it into the top pocket of his shirt.

"All in order, Mr. Belasko," he said, handing back the passport. "Enjoy your stay on Cielo. If there's anything I can do, just ask for Captain Varro."

Bolan took the passport. "I'll remember that, Captain."

Benares was given the same treatment, as was Lang when he returned to the cabin.

After the three cops had gone Lang said, "I need some fresh air, guys."

They went up on deck and stood surveying the crowded bay area. It was a mix of hotels and casinos. Beyond the buildings Bolan could see the rich vegetation that was natural to the island.

From Lang, Bolan had learned that Cielo was roughly seventy miles long by thirty at its widest point. A small mountain range ran from south to north, with untouched areas of near-tropical forest dominating the central area. There was a little farming and some local industry. The bulk of the small population lived on the coast, with fishing and tourism the major industries. It boasted a small airfield. International flights touched down on the Colombian mainland, and shuttles carried the tourists to Cielo.

The latest intel from Stony Man Farm was that the physicist, Dr. Ralph Semple, had been seen leaving on a flight for Colombia. Later, Bob Lang had relayed additional information. Semple had taken a flight from Colombia to Cielo. Lang's local informant had kept a close watch on the doctor's movements. On the afternoon of his second day on Cielo, Semple had been picked up outside his hotel by a car from Dupre's estate. That had been two days earlier. Semple hadn't returned to his hotel. It appeared that the doctor was a full-time guest of Dupre's.

"Bob, I need to talk to your man," Bolan said.

Lang led the way along the dock. A number of taxis were lined up along the sidewalk. Lang opened the rear door of a gaudily painted, elderly Buick. Bolan followed the DEA man into the car.

The agent leaned forward and tapped the driver on the shoulder.

"Give us the guided tour," he said.

The cab rolled away from the curb.

"Belasko, this is Gabriel Lorenz."

The driver raised his eyes to the rearview mirror and nodded to Bolan.

"You're enjoying Cielo?" he asked.

"The entry fee's pretty high."

Lorenz chuckled, showing gold teeth.

"You're talking about Captain Varro. I remember when he was nothing more than a traffic cop. When he sold out to the cartel, his promotion was rapid. To repay his loyalty, the cartel gave him charge of the police force here on Cielo, to protect their interests and also to line his own pocket. Watch out for him. He is a bad one."

"Gabe, can you update Belasko on the situation at Dupre's estate?"

"All I know is that Semple is still there. Is this man important?"

"If and when the time comes, I'll give you more," Bolan said. "It's a need-to-know on this one."

The driver shrugged. "I understand."

They drove into the countryside, cruising the main highway, the blue water of the Caribbean visible through the trees and lush vegetation.

Forty minutes later Lorenz pulled the cab to a stop on a high point overlooking the coastline. They'd left the main highway, taking a lesser road that brought them to the observation point. Lang led the way past a couple of wooden benches to a telescope mounted on a dais.

"Go to the right and down," the agent instructed Bolan, "beyond that last clump of trees."

The soldier put his eye to the instrument. Dupre's estate came into sharp relief. Bolan scanned the perimeter, the large main house and the outbuildings. At the rear was a large swimming pool, next to that tennis courts. A helipad stood on the coast side of the house, unoccupied at the moment.

"Gabe can provide you with details of the estate," Lang said as they returned to the cab.

"I'd appreciate anything you can tell me," Bolan said.

"Sure. What in particular?" Lorenz asked.

Bolan leaned forward. "Two things. How to get in, and what I need to know to stay alive while I'm there."

17

"Is there any possibility Varro, or any of the cartel people, might suspect you guys are DEA?" Bolan asked.

It was evening. The air was warm and breezy, carrying the faint scent of flowers. They sat on the deck of the cruiser. Lights from the casinos and bars threw shimmering reflections across the water of Cielo Bay.

Bob Lang lit a thin cigar, considering Bolan's question.

"I can't say for sure, Belasko. For all we know these people could've gotten the make on us the first time we sailed in here. They could be playing a damn game with us, letting us pick up little bits of information so we can feed it back to Washington and keep our people happy."

"On the other hand," Benares suggested, "they could still believe we're who we say we are, and they'll go on taking our money at the casinos. The nice part of that is we're gambling with cartel money.

Every dime we spend comes from cash confiscated from busts we've made."

"I don't want to do anything that could compromise either of you," Bolan said. "I play by different rules. No running back to Washington and asking for permission. If I see a need, I do what's necessary, on the spot. No comebacks, just results. If I go in and Dupre's people get in my way..."

"Don't sweat it, Belasko," Benares said. "We understand. We're no rookies. When it comes down to it, we're cops doing a job. One bad guy is like any other."

In the early hours of the morning, Bolan and Lang stood outside a casino, looking for all the world like a pair of high rollers out for a breath of air. They'd spent a few hours in the casino, mingling with the crowds, playing at a few tables. Now they were waiting at the curb, still acting their parts. When Gabe Lorenz pulled his cab alongside, Lang bent over, leaning his hands on the roof as he spoke to the driver.

"My favorite cabbie. Me and my buddy want to find a couple of nice ladies."

They got into the cab and Lorenz cruised down the street.

"There's a carryall under the seat," he said. "All the stuff you guys wanted. What you aiming to do, start a war?"

Lang pulled out the bag and placed it on the rear seat between himself and Bolan. He opened the zipper.

"Just fighting the same one," Bolan said.

In the bag were handguns and a couple of 9 mm Uzis, with extra magazines for the weapons, a sheathed knife and a number of stun grenades.

Bolan stripped off his light shirt. Underneath he wore a black T-shirt to match his black pants. He pulled on one of the shoulder rigs from the bag and checked the Beretta Model 92 pistol before leathering it in the holster. He then pulled on a black windbreaker.

They were already beyond Cielo Bay, following the coastal road that would take them to Dupre's estate.

Similarly clad, Lang loaded both Uzi subguns, then leaned back, watching the dark coastline slip by.

"You sure you don't want me to hang around to pick you up?" Lorenz asked.

"Yeah. You get back to Cielo Bay," Bolan said. "Benares will pick us up in the cruiser. He should be in position within the next thirty minutes."

Lorenz dropped them half a mile from the estate. They waited until the cab's taillights winked out of sight around a bend, then left the road and pushed their way through the thick foliage. Lang knew the terrain, and he guided Bolan through the deep shadows.

They reached the perimeter of the estate. Lang's information had the place surrounded by a wall and security cameras. Crouching in the darkness at the base of the wall, they were able to confirm that the intel was correct.

"Any ideas?" Lang asked.

Bolan didn't answer. He scanned the wall and studied the swiveling camera that covered the section they were in. Then he moved along and did a similar check on the next camera.

"The cameras cover the top of the wall and the areas below," he said, on his return.

"That's what I'd expect them to cover. What's your point, Belasko?"

Bolan only smiled. He moved back into the dense foliage and peered up into the branches of a tree that stood some yards away from the wall. Lang watched him. The soldier slung the Uzi, then reached for the lowest branches of the tree and pulled himself up. Silently he climbed into the highest branches, chose one that extended out toward the wall and began to edge along it. Lang watched in silence, Bolan's plan finally dawning on him.

He saw Bolan reach the outermost branch. It began to sag with his weight, curving gently down in an arc that dropped the Executioner over the top of the wall, above the security camera. The moment the branch reached the limit of its arc, Bolan let himself hang by his hands. He swung for a few seconds, then launched himself into the shadows beyond the wall.

Lang slung his Uzi and followed Bolan's actions. He made it to the upper branches, shuffling his way along the one the soldier had used. He felt a moment of panic as the branch began to bend, but controlled himself and let his body down. Dangling by his hands, he peered into the dark beyond the wall. For a moment he couldn't see a thing, then he heard Bolan's voice, floating up from the ground.

"Let's go, Lang."

The agent took a breath and released his grip on the branch. He hit the ground, rolled and felt Bolan grab his arm as he got to his feet.

"This way," Bolan said and set off toward a thick stand of shrubs.

"Keep your eyes open for roving security guards," he said.

"Lorenz said they carry out irregular patrols, so we're not going to get much warning. The house has floodlights around it. And watch out for more cameras."

They used the landscaped garden as cover, moving from bush to bush, tree to tree, dodging the security cameras, until they were able to crouch behind an ornamental fountain and study the sprawling mass of the main house. During their silent approach they'd spotted two armed guards pacing the smooth lawns. One they'd caught at a distance. The other had passed within a yard of where they'd hidden behind the thick trunk of a tree. As the guard moved by them, Bolan saw that he carried a transceiver clipped to his belt. He was also armed with a heavy autopistol and carried a bulky combat shotgun.

The house was a large, two-storied structure. They were facing the frontage. Powerful floodlights, set back from the building, bathed it in light. To the right, and jutting from the house, were garages, with quarters built over them. According to Lorenz's information, that was where the estate's security contingent was housed.

"Access to the beach should be that way," Lang said, pointing.

"We'll check it out first," Bolan replied. "I don't want last-minute problems if we have to leave in a hurry."

They skirted the house, angling around to the rear. There was a large, paved patio area, and beyond that lay the swimming pool. Steps on the extreme edge of the patio led down to the beach. A stone jetty pushed out into the sea, with a number of powerboats moored alongside.

Bolan scanned the area. More floodlights bathed the rear of the house. It seemed that Colonel Dupre wasn't very comfortable in the dark.

"All this, for a bastard like Dupre," Lang said. "He tore his country apart, slaughtered his people and then jumped ship with half the national wealth. And while he's here, he can't be touched."

"The rules are changed tonight," Bolan replied.

He cut back toward the house, followed by Lang. They watched their backs as they moved in, dodging the cameras that were designed to monitor a specific area in a controlled arc, leaving brief blind spots that they used to their advantage.

They were close to the main structure when a guard stepped out of the shadows ahead of them.

He froze for a moment, his mouth half open in surprise. His left hand dropped to the transceiver on his belt, the other lifting the shotgun he carried.

Bolan, no more than a few feet from the man, moved with a speed that Lang barely registered. The Executioner's right arm swept up, smashing across the guard's throat with enough power to lift the man off his feet and drop him flat on his back. He landed hard, the breath knocked from his lungs. The shotgun spilled from his fingers. The man tried to rise, but Bolan swung the side of his foot into the guard's face, sending his head back to rap against the ground. His body arched once, then went limp.

The Executioner disarmed him, tossing the pistol and shotgun into a nearby bush. Turning, he waved Lang in.

"The way these guys operate, it could be five minutes or an hour before they miss this one. I want to get inside now."

"What do you want me to do?"

"Keep your eyes open. Let me know if we're spotted."

"You got it, pal."

"Lang, remember what I said earlier. No rule book on this one. If it goes hard, don't forget who these guys are. They tortured and killed for Dupre, including women and children. Don't go soft on me."

Lang nodded. "No chance of that, Belasko."

Bolan turned toward the house, his Uzi unslung.

"Belasko!"

Lang's warning yell brought Bolan around in a tight crouch, the Uzi tracking ahead of him.

He saw Lang—one hand thrown out to warn Bolan back, his other bringing his own weapon into play.

The agent was between the Executioner and a line of armed hardmen who'd come out of concealment. They were silhouetted against the glare of powerful spotlights that had suddenly burst into life. The white light burned into Bolan's eyes, forcing him to turn his head to try to maintain a semblance of vision.

"Resist and you will die right now, Belasko!"

The voice came from the line of men.

"Believe me, there is no way you can win."

Bolan accepted the man's logic. There were too many of them, their weapons up and gleaming dully. He could make out more than a dozen, and maybe more out of his sight. He allowed the Uzi to slip from his hands.

"Sensible," the man said, detaching himself from the others and moving toward the agent. "I hope Lang sees the situation in the same way."

"Do as he says, Lang. This isn't the time," Bolan said.

The agent began to lower his weapon, until the advancing figure reached him.

Bolan heard the DEA man groan, a sound of despair and disillusionment.

Then Lang gave a wild yell of anger and yanked the Uzi back into target acquisition.

"Lousy son of a bitch!"

The dark figure barely paused. He swiveled at the hips, his right hand raising the heavy pistol he'd been concealing at his side.

There was a single shot, a powerful, heavy sound as the weapon spit, the muzzle no more than three feet from Lang's head. The slug burned deep into his skull and erupted from the other end in a dark spray. Lang was thrown to the ground, his body going into spasms.

The killer pulled his weapon around, leveling it at Bolan, his finger against the trigger. He moved forward, turning slightly so the light played across his face.

"You want the same way out, Belasko?" Gabriel Lorenz asked, smiling.

18

"You wanted to see inside my house," Colonel Jules Dupre said. "Welcome, Mr. Belasko, I invite you to accompany me on a tour. I believe I know what you have come to see."

The former dictator was an imposing figure. He stood over six feet tall. He was broad and powerfully built, although the hardness of his frame had been softened somewhat by the idle life he was forced to live on Cielo. There was a hint of flesh around the jaw, a fullness around his waist, but the cruel gleam still showed in his eyes.

Bolan stood in the center of the large room, surrounded by armed men, Dupre's Black Skulls. The death squad had terrorized an entire nation back on St. Maritan. The Executioner had no doubt they would kill him in an instant. All it would take was a flick of Dupre's manicured fingers. He stayed silent, under control, but his anger showed in his eyes when he spotted Gabriel Lorenz coming back into the room. The traitor crossed to join Dupre, avoiding Bolan's eyes.

"Well?" Dupre demanded.

"Captain Varro has dealt with the other American."

"The good guys are losing tonight," Dupre said, looking at Bolan. "Not very encouraging, Belasko."

The soldier kept his gaze on Lorenz. Dupre picked up on the tension and chuckled.

"I don't envy your chances of surviving very long, Lorenz, if you find yourself too close to Belasko."

Lorenz scowled. "Give me a gun and I'll finish him now."

There was a snort from one of Dupre's bodyguards.

"Put them in a room together," he suggested.

"That's not very sporting," Dupre said. "After all, if Lorenz hadn't spent all that time feeding information to our DEA friends, we might not have learned about Mr. Belasko."

"They must have paid you well, Lorenz," Bolan said. "What's the going rate for betrayal?"

"It pays extremely well," Dupre replied. "In cartel terms, a mere handful of change. To Lorenz, a fortune. I find it fascinating how each person values money, and what they do to earn it."

"Spend it quickly, Lorenz," Bolan said. "You don't have a lot of time left."

"Damn you!" Lorenz roared. He lunged at Bolan, his right hand snatching the pistol from his belt.

Bolan watched Lorenz bring his weapon to bear and knew no one would do a thing to stop the traitor.

As the muzzle rose, the Executioner took a step forward, turning his body toward Lorenz. He caught the man's gun hand, pulling and twisting at the same time. Lorenz was slammed hard against Bolan's hip, his gun hand forced towards the ceiling. The soldier's left arm snaked around his neck, pushing back. Lorenz began to struggle, panic setting in as he felt the pressure building up against his spine. His finger tightened on the trigger, and the pistol exploded with a loud roar. The bullet slammed into the ceiling, showering plaster on the room.

The last sound Lorenz ever made was lost in the crack of the shot. The warrior exerted a final push, snapping the man's spine. Lorenz slid from his grasp and thudded to the floor, Bolan still retaining his grip on the man's gun hand.

The rattle of weapons reached his ears.

"Think about your next move very carefully, Belasko," Dupre warned.

Bolan let go of the dead man's hand, and his arm flopped to the floor.

"Very wise." Dupre picked up the gun and looked at Bolan.

"And very impressive."

"I don't kill to impress people."

"Yes, I can believe that. No matter, you saved me doing the job myself. A man who betrays once can never be trusted. He served his purpose."

Dupre tossed the handgun to one of his men.

"Come with me," he ordered the Executioner.

Bolan followed him through the house, Dupre's armed bodyguards bringing up in the rear.

"You have great persistence, Belasko," Dupre said. "I've been monitoring your progress. I have been informed that Mason Sheppard died trying to prevent you from escaping from Russia. He should have had you killed the moment you appeared in Scotland. That was his mistake and he paid for it. Despite your interference, he did manage to complete his part of the contract and send me my merchandise."

"Why don't we stop playing games, Dupre? We both know we're talking about a nuclear bomb."

"Very well. The components for the bomb are now in my hands. They are being analyzed at this very moment prior to being assembled and shipped off."

"By Dr. Ralph Semple?"

"Again you are extremely well-informed. Yes, Dr. Semple has agreed to take care of the bomb when it reaches its destination. He will accompany it, of course, and see to its placement. It's surprising the amount of work to be done, right up to the last few hours. Semple will be there to make sure no last-minute hitches occur."

"I suppose there's no point asking you where that might be?"

"None at all."

"Do you really believe you can get away with this?"

"Why not? I have the components. True, it has taken me over two years to bring them all together, but that is all behind me now. The next few days will bring it to a successful conclusion."

They reached the end of a long, tiled passage. Dupre paused before a heavy door. A keypad was set into the wall beside it. Dupre moved to it, shielding the pad from Bolan with his body as he keyed in a number sequence. There was a click from the door as security bolts snapped back. The door opened at Dupre's pull.

"I think you will find this interesting."

Bolan, followed by Dupre's hardmen, went through the door and down a concrete ramp. He found himself in a medium-sized room. Fluorescent light bounced off the white walls. Work surfaces held a variety of analytical instruments. There was also a computer workstation. In the center of the room stood a square bench unit. Over it hung a powerful lamp, throwing clean, brilliant light onto the unit.

Perched on a high stool, hunching over the work surface, was Dr. Semple. His attention was focused on a component laid before him, the object Bolan had been following halfway across the world.

The nuclear bomb casing gleamed with a cold light, its surface smooth and polished.

"Dr. Semple," Dupre said, "a brief interruption."

Semple glanced up. His face was pale, and there were dark rings under his eyes. He looked exhausted.

"I could do with a break."

He eased off the stool, stretching his tall, spare frame as he crossed to help himself to a mug of coffee from a bubbling percolator. He turned, leaning against the edge of the work surface.

"So this is Belasko."

Dupre nodded. "I felt generous. I decided Mr. Belasko should see your wonderful creation. He has made such an effort to end our plans I thought he should be allowed to at least see what it was all about before he dies."

"Not in here, I hope," Semple said.

"Of course not." Dupre glanced at Bolan. "You do realize I cannot allow you to live any longer? You are a threat, and as long as you are alive, you will continue to be one. We are too close to success to allow anything to interfere."

Bolan didn't respond. He turned to the work surface, scanning the material laid out there.

"Fascinating, isn't it?" Semple said, moving to stand on the far side of the bench.

"By tomorrow it'll be on its way. When it arrives on-site I'll check it, prime it, then leave the rest to the colonel's team."

"As simple as that," Bolan said.

"As nuclear devices go, this one is crude, I admit, but sophistication isn't required in this case. A sphere of uranium 235 goes in here," he said, touching the main bowl of the casing. "A second piece, formed like a large bullet, goes in the barrel above it. Behind that is an explosive propellant. A detonator will fire the propellant and the resultant energy will send the 235 bullet into the main sphere, down a central pathway. When the two sections of 235 come together, the impact will create a runaway chain reaction and subsequent nuclear explosion."

"What kind of power are we talking about?"

"The main sphere of 235 weighs around 25 kilos. It will produce an explosion equivalent to thirteen hundred tons of TNT. That's only one-tenth of the Hiroshima bomb, but it's still a big bang."

"You have the uranium here, too?" Bolan asked.

Semple nodded. "In a safe storage container." He smiled. "Unfortunately I can't show you that. It's extremely dangerous material."

"It'll be a lot more dangerous when you detonate it."

"That's the idea. This device isn't being constructed for show. It's going to be used."

"That doesn't bother you?"

"No. Why should it? People are dying every day. A few more aren't going to make much difference."

"Mass murder's well paid these days, isn't it?"

"As a matter of fact, it is," the doctor replied. "Don't try to analyze me, Belasko. I know what I'm doing, and my reasons are purely financial. I abandoned ethics and morals a long time ago. I'm basically a product of my birthright. Knowledge and expertise for monetary gain. When this is over I can go anywhere and do anything I want."

"We have created a world of supply and demand, Belasko," Dupre said. "I needed something that Dr. Semple could supply. He, in turn, wanted to leave his mediocre life behind and have the freedom to go where he wanted. Our mutual needs brought us together. We both get what we want."

"And what is that?"

"You are full of questions, Belasko. I do believe you will be asking them right up to the moment of your death."

"You can bet on that."

Semple banged down his coffee mug. "Get him out of here. The sooner you dispose of him, the better. He's trouble, Dupre."

"I am inclined to agree with you. We will leave you to your work, Doctor."

Bolan was manhandled out of the room.

Dupre paused as the door closed behind them.

"Take him out to the garage," he ordered his bodyguards. "Do it there and then dispose of the body." He turned to Bolan. "There is no easy way to say it, Belasko."

Bolan didn't answer. He wasn't going to give Dupre the satisfaction of a reply.

The ex-dictator walked away, leaving Bolan alone with his potential executioners. There were four of them, all armed with subguns. The soldier had no doubt they were fully experienced in summary slayings. It had been their stock-in-trade back on St. Maritan. They wouldn't have lost their skills, despite being confined to this semiparadise.

"Move out," one of them ordered. He prodded Bolan in the ribs with the barrel of his weapon.

They moved back along the passage. When they reached a side door, one of the bodyguards unlocked it. Bolan was pushed through. He found himself in a concreted area at the side of the house.

Through strategically placed bushes he could see the gleam of the swimming pool.

"Around that way," he was instructed.

Bolan allowed himself to be guided, his mind focused on coming up with some kind of plan, a diversion that would offer him a chance to break free, but nothing seemed to be forthcoming.

The garage block appeared ahead of them. One of the guards went ahead and opened the access door. As they passed a window, Bolan glanced inside. The interior was only partly lit, but enough for him to see a line of polished cars standing in a row. He was pushed inside the garage.

"Where do you want to do this?" one of the guards asked.

The man in charge waved a hand in the direction of the rear of the building.

"Over in the corner. We don't want any mess by the cars."

The exchange had taken only a few seconds. Bolan didn't waste them.

A flick of his eyes showed the panel of light switches to be to his right, no more than a couple of feet away. Only one switch was in the on position.

A big hand grasped Bolan's shoulder.

"Let's go."

The Executioner took a step forward, bringing him level with the bank of switches.

His right hand darted out, a finger clicking off the switch, plunging the garage into darkness.

He didn't go for the door. It was too far and blocked by the other guards.

In the confusion created by the sudden darkness, he moved to the left and dropped to the concrete floor. He rolled under the closest car, then kept on moving, rolling beneath the line of vehicles until he was at the far end of the row against the wall. Pushing to his feet, he crouched as the lights were switched on.

There was a babble of excited, angry voices as the guards argued over what to do.

Bolan used the time to move to the rear of the car he'd used as cover.

A workbench stood against the wall to his left, and above that was a board with various tools used to service the fleet of vehicles.

There were a number of flat, solid tire irons. Bolan crept to the bench, reached up and slid two of them from their clips.

The agitated voices had calmed a bit. The guard in charge was dispersing his cohorts. Bolan heard the scuff of shoes on concrete as they spread out across the garage. He dropped to the floor again, peering under the car chassis and monitoring the movement of the feet in his line of vision.

One pair moved quickly along the rear, heading directly for Bolan's position. the Executioner stayed prone, waiting until the gunner reached the last car in the row.

As the man stepped slowly around the rear of the vehicle, coming into view, Bolan erupted from the floor. The tire irons in his hands were a blur as he lashed out with them. He connected with the guard's neck, just below his left ear, putting every ounce of strength into the blow. The guard slumped to one side. Before he could respond Bolan drove the second iron against his head, shattering the skull, driving shards of bone into his brain. The guard stiffened and crashed to the floor.

Bolan snatched up the discarded Uzi.

He sensed movement at the front of the car. Spinning, the Uzi up and tracking, he saw another armed figure. He triggered the weapon, sending a burst of slugs into the guard's chest. The hardman fell back with a brief cry of surprise, blood gleaming on his shirt.

The warrior caught the crackle of a weapon a split second before a stream of bullets blew out both sets of windows of the car he was using for cover. The line of slugs followed him as he dived to the floor at the rear of the vehicle. He rolled to the side and braced himself against the wall. Peering along the ground, he saw the lower legs and feet of a bodyguard. He lowered the Uzi's muzzle and triggered a short burst. The man screamed as 9 mm slugs blasted through his ankles. He fell to the floor, writhing in agony, involuntarily triggering his weapon and blasting a burst of rounds through the gas tank of the nearest car.

As the pungent odor of gasoline began to spread through the garage, Bolan scrambled to his feet, eyes searching the far side of the building. There was still one of the bodyguards up and running. He heard the door crash open as the man dodged outside. It would take him only a minute to raise the alarm. Once that happened the grounds would be crawling with armed guards.

Bolan checked out the two untouched cars. Neither had a key in the ignition. He didn't have time to hot-wire one. The last thing he needed was to become trapped inside the garage, surrounded by Dupre's armed heavies.

Passing the workbench, he spotted a butane blowtorch. It was ignited by pressing a tab on the side. He picked it up, moving quickly to the rear of the garage and the exit door. He released the bolts, lit the blowtorch and touched it to the pool of fuel spreading across the floor. The flames leapt away from him, rising swiftly toward the punctured gas tank. He scooped up a second discarded Uzi, then took a full length dive through the door and into the darkness the instant the gas tank erupted.

Gaining his feet, Bolan ran, skirting the swimming pool and edging around the tennis courts.

Two more explosions sounded behind him. He glanced back and saw that the garage had vanished in a burst of orange flame. Thick clouds of smoke billowed skyward.

Raised voices reached his ears as he pushed on, seeking the cover of the trees that edged the southern perimeter of the estate. Beyond that lay the shoreline.

The crackle of gunfire split the night. The shots were wide of their mark, and Bolan heard them thunk into the ground. He pushed up a gentle slope and broke into the cover of the tree line. The ground beneath his feet was soft and spongy. The fire behind him threw enough light to repel the darkness within the trees, making it easier for him to find his way.

Voices came from off to his right.

Bolan paused, taking a moment to remove the magazine from the second Uzi. He tucked it behind his belt and tossed the weapon far into the distance. Seconds later the sound of weapons pinpointed his pursuers, as they let loose on his diversionary tactic.

He headed off in the opposite direction. Almost without warning he stepped out from the tree line and found he was on the edge of the mainland. Only a low fence separated him from the edge and the steep, ragged slope that ran down to the beach twenty feet below.

His two pursuers reached the same point moments later, emerging from the trees just yards away from him.

Bolan heard them coming and brought the Uzi around, targeting them the minute they appeared.

The pair reacted by raising their own weapons and sighting on their enemy.

The Executioner cut loose with a ferocious burst, his figure-eight pattern drilling into the bodyguards. They were driven to the ground as one, their limbs windmilling in bloody agony.

Shouldering his weapon, Bolan climbed the fence and made his way down the slope, leaning back against the gradient and digging his heels into the soft earth. His passage loosened a shower of earth and rocks that threatened to drag him with them, and he fought to maintain his balance.

He paused long enough at the bottom to get a fix on his position. His way back to Cielo Bay would be west, but he had no reason to return. Bob Lang and Sol Benares were dead, so he had no contacts waiting there. By now the cruiser would have been taken over by Captain Varro and his men. It would undoubtedly be staked out, once Dupre informed the police captain that Bolan had escaped.

The soldier made his way along the beach until he reached a natural breakwater. He climbed in among the rocks, finding a spot where he could see in all directions. He knew Dupre would have every man on his payroll out looking for him. The colonel's plan depended on secrecy, the shock value attached to such a venture. Any leak would alert authorities worldwide. Smuggling the nuclear device into the chosen country would be difficult enough, but with everyone on full alert, Dupre would have the odds raised significantly. The colonel needed a complete clampdown. If he could smuggle his bomb to its destination under cover of secrecy, then his scheme was already on its way to a successful end.

The roar of an engine swept away these thoughts from Bolan's mind. He turned to locate the source and saw the bright headlights of a wide-tired beach buggy come into view round the headland. The vehicle bounced across the sand, heading directly for the soldier's position.

An armed man stood beside the driver, braced against the sway of the buggy, resting the barrel of his automatic weapon across the roll bar. The gunner triggered his subgun, sending a stream of 9 mm slugs toward Bolan.

The Executioner hit the sand facedown, then rolled over. He tracked in on the buggy's front tire and sent out a blast of fire. The thick rubber shredded, blowing out with a bang. The cumbersome vehicle, suddenly deprived of its forward motion, executed a roll, throwing driver and gunner clear.

Bolan got to his feet and faced the gunner as the man stood up. His weapon stitched a bloody row of holes in the gunner's chest, throwing him back to the ground. This time he stayed down.

Hearing the snap of a slide being pulled back, the soldier dropped to a crouch, swinging the Uzi around. He triggered the machine pistol a fraction ahead of the driver, his burst caving in the front of his adversary's face and sending a red stream onto the sand. The driver pitched over, giving a grunt before falling silent.

Bolan moved swiftly to the overturned buggy. He needed to see if he could increase his arsenal.

He needed all the help he could get.

19

Bolan heard a second buggy approaching. It slewed around the headland, the beams of its lights silhouetting him as he cut across the beach.

The vehicle lurched to a stop, spilling four armed men to the ground. Shouted orders spread the bodyguards out in a ragged line, and they started to follow Bolan along the beach. Out on the water, a powerboat began to run parallel to the shore, the powerful searchlight mounted on its deck throwing a beam of light over the sand. It swept back and forth, searching for its quarry.

Bolan went prone, facing the oncoming bodyguards. Beside him lay the extra weapons he'd pulled from the wrecked buggy: a long-barrel Uzi with a double magazine and a Colt Python revolver.

He could hear the throb of the powerboat. It had moved closer to shore, the operator still scanning the beach with his searchlight. Bolan reached out and pulled the handgun closer. He wanted that searchlight out of operation before he took on the bodyguards. Any illumination would help them as much as it helped him.

He checked the line of men again. They seemed to be holding back, unable to home in on his position. They glanced around as they deliberated what their next move should be.

The Executioner picked up the Python, swiveling to face the boat. It was almost level with him, and within range of the powerful handgun. Resting both elbows on the sand, Bolan took aim, centering the muzzle on the searchlight. He triggered two quick shots and heard the muffled burst of sound as the light went out.

The moment he'd fired, he turned back and snatched up the Uzi. He rolled away from his original position, only moments ahead of the vicious stream of slugs that burrowed into the sand. Flat on his stomach he angled the Uzi up at the Black Skulls who were converging on his former position. He triggered the weapon, scything the advancing hardmen with a deadly volley. He took two out with his initial burst, then saw the others break off and go in separate directions.

Bolan got up on one knee, tracking the bodyguard closest to him. The man moved in a wide circle, trying to come up on Bolan's blind side, but he made the mistake of moving parallel with the water, and his shape was sharply outlined against the night sky as it was reflected off the water. Bolan triggered the Uzi and saw the figure stop in his tracks before throwing his arms wide and toppling into the water.

The solid crackle of an automatic weapon drew Bolan's attention to the surviving bodyguard. The gunner had picked up on his enemy, and he came in fast, weaving as he ran. He began to fire, his shots creeping closer as he found the range. Bolan felt something hit hard on the underside of his left arm, and the spread of warm blood told him he'd taken a hit.

He blotted out the pain, concentrating his complete attention on the oncoming bodyguard. He raised the Uzi, made target acquisition and rattled out the final half dozen 9 mm slugs.

The bodyguard stumbled and fell facedown in the sand, dark patches staining the back of his shirt where the slugs had emerged. The hardman groaned, then rolled onto his side, fumbling for the handgun tucked into a hip holster. He yanked out the big pistol, pushing up off the sand with his free hand, the muzzle seeking a target.

Bolan moved to his opponent's blind side. He ejected the spent magazine and snapped in a fresh one. Pulling back the bolt, he cocked the weapon and triggered a short burst into the man as he started to bring the pistol on line. The bodyguard rolled onto his back and didn't move again.

Snatching up the second Uzi and the Python, the Executioner headed down the beach. His mind had been at work all through the confrontation with Dupre's bodyguards, seeking a way out, something that would enable him to get away. His best bet was just off-shore—the powerboat.

Bolan didn't know how many were on board, but he had two things in his favor: they wouldn't be expecting an attack from land, and with its searchlight out of action, the boat was slightly more vulnerable.

He reached the water's edge and waded in, feeling the drag of the current as he eased out from shore.

The powerboat appeared to be waiting, perhaps for some signal from Dupre's land-based bodyguards.

When the sea reached chest height, Bolan made sure that both Uzis were securely slung around his neck, while he held the Python clear of the water. As he neared the stern of the boat, he felt the turbulence created by the craft's propeller.

He moved to the seaward side of the craft, having to tread water now, the darkness helping to conceal his approach.

As he eased alongside the vessel, he came across a rope hanging over the side. He used it to pull himself tight against the sleek hull. Water lapped against the craft as it rose and fell with the water's swell. Listening for any sound that might indicate the position of the boat's crew, Bolan knew that he was going to have to make a move. Sooner or later the crew would realize there was no one left alive on the beach.

He reached up with his left hand and clamped it around the brass rail that ran around the deck. He pulled himself up out of the warm water until he was able to see over the rail.

Three men were huddled around the smashed searchlight that was mounted on a metal swivel. They were discussing some matter in a foreign tongue, speaking too fast for Bolan to comprehend. He dragged himself on board, dropping silently to the deck.

He picked up the soft sound of a footfall behind him, overridden by the metallic click of a handgun being cocked. He twisted and rolled hearing the blast of the weapon and feeling the vibration of the slug as it hit the deck. Wood splinters bounced off his clothing. He pushed the Colt forward, muzzle up and tracking, and triggered a single .357 slug into the broad torso of the man looming over him. The target fell back, toppling over a length of coiled rope.

Bolan pushed to his feet, hearing the sudden commotion from the men gathered by the searchlight. Someone fired a handgun, flashes winking in the darkness.

The Executioner sprang up on the closest hatch cover. He slid across it and dropped to the deck on the far side. He stayed down, below the level of the hatch, as he crept forward, monitoring the frantic actions of the crew members.

A man began to yell, his words falling over themselves as he gave vent to his anger. His tirade as well as the response he got was delivered in the foreign language he'd heard earlier, but Bolan understood the intent—they were pushing one another into making some kind of move.

Bolan rounded the front of the main cabin and spotted one of the crewmen, pressed flat against the superstructure on the opposite side of the boat. The man turned just as the soldier appeared. He locked eyes with the Executioner and let loose with his pistol. He returned fire, driving a Magnum slug into the man's heart. It punched him backward over the rail and into the sea.

Dropping the Python to the deck, Bolan unslung the Uzi. He heard the soft pad of deck shoes overhead and realized that one of the crew was on the cabin roof. He flattened against the cabin's frontage. When the man leaned over the edge of the roof and peered onto the deck, Bolan triggered a burst from the Uzi that tore through the man's jaw and blasted into his skull. The crewman went over as if he'd been struck by lightning.

Bolan eased over to the far corner of the cabin and checked out the stern. He heard the soft splash of water against the hull, while beneath his feet the idling engine continued to throb.

The scrape of a door being opened caught his attention. Bolan leaned out and glanced up. He was rewarded by the sight of a shadow moving behind the glass and knew he had his man pinpointed in the wheelhouse.

He catfooted around to the door, which stood ajar, allowing him to peer inside. The figure hunched over the boat's radio held a .357 Magnum Desert Eagle in his free hand.

Bolan tapped on the doorframe with the barrel of the Uzi to attract the man's attention.

"Leave it," he said. "Leave the radio."

The soldier didn't know whether the gunner understood what he'd said.

The man spun away from the radio, firing his pistol the same instant Bolan stroked the Uzi's trigger.

The .357 Magnum slug blew out a large chunk from the doorframe just above Bolan's head, but then the 9 mm bullets from the Uzi chewed a bloody, ragged line from the man's groin to his throat. He flailed his arms wildly as he dropped to the floor. The Desert Eagle fell from his fingers, thumping when it struck the deck.

The soldier leaned against the doorframe. He could still feel blood running from the deep gash in his arm. Locating the first-aid locker, he fashioned a makeshift pressure pad and bound it tightly against the wound. Once he had the bandage in place, he turned his attention to more pressing matters. He needed to take the boat away from its position and lose it in one of the numerous coves that dotted the coastline.

He hauled in the anchor and returned to the wheelhouse. He eased the throttle open and turned the vessel toward the open water. Once clear of the area, he increased his speed, following the uneven coastline. He refrained from putting on any running lights in case he gave away his position. For all he knew Dupre might have other boats in the vicinity, so it would be wise to keep a low profile.

The farther he traveled from the Colonel's estate, the wilder the coastline became. He was moving up toward the less inhabited section of the island, which would offer him a better chance of remaining free while he worked out his next move.

Bolan realized dawn wasn't far off. He guided the boat closer to shore, searching for a good place to hide it.

He soon found a suitable inlet, thickly overhanging foliage shielding it from view. He eased the craft through the curtain of greenery, which fell back into place behind him. He kept to the center of the channel, avoiding the thick foliage and close-standing trees that crowded the banks. After a couple of dozen yards, the inlet curved to the right. Bolan steered the boat around the bend and felt the keel scrape bottom, telling him that the channel was shallowing out. He steered into the bank and cut the motor. Taking the stern line, he hitched it around the trunk of a nearby tree. Then he returned to the boat.

The moment he relaxed he felt exhaustion hit him—the result of loss of blood from his arm wound and the battles he'd fought. He gathered his weapons and took them below deck. In the small galley, he found water in a storage bottle. He tipped some into a pan and put it on the butane stove to heat. Rummaging in a cupboard, he found a jar of instant coffee and spooned some into a china mug.

While the water boiled, he tended to his arm again. As he cleaned the wound, he saw that the ragged tear was deep. It was going to need stitching sooner or later. He put on some antiseptic ointment, then applied a fresh pad and rebound the wound. Pulling his shirt back on, he turned his mind back to the mission.

Gabriel Lorenz's betrayal had turned everything around, forcing Bolan to abandon his initial plan to destroy or incapacitate the bomb in order to simply survive. He'd managed that. Now he had to turn the tables on Dupre and Semple.

The rogue physicist was an essential key to Dupre's plan. When the bomb was transported to its final destination, it would be Semple who primed and set the device. Without Semple, the operation would be suspended. Dupre wasn't going to find a replacement very easily. Removing Semple might not put a complete stop to the colonel's scheme, but it would delay it—and once his plan was made public, Dupre would be left out on a limb.

The pan of water began to boil. Getting to his feet, Bolan poured the boiled water into the mug, stirring the brew as he made his way to a table set in the middle of the cabin.

The boat rocked gently. Bolan could hear the hull rubbing against the bank, picked up the soft pinging of metal as the motor cooled. He drank some of the hot coffee, feeling it course down his throat. The atmosphere lulled him. He tried to fight off the weariness by drinking more coffee. The hot liquid revived him briefly, but the tiredness came over him again and he leaned his head against the bulkhead. His eyes felt heavy and he succumbed to sleep.

BOLAN'S EYES SNAPPED OPEN. He reached for the Uzi he'd placed on the table close at hand. He fisted the weapon and turned to the open door. A slight figure stood there clad in cotton whites.

The man spoke a local Spanish dialect that Bolan had difficulty translating. He raised his free hand, waving it gently.

"I'm American. Do you speak English?"

"A little," the man said, gesturing with his thumb and forefinger held slightly apart. "My name is Escobar."

"Where am I exactly?" Bolan asked. "What is this place?"

Escobar listened puzzled, as Bolan repeated his questions. The Executioner then raised his hand, indicating he wanted the man to follow him. They made their way to the wheelhouse where Bolan unearthed a large map of Cielo Island.

"This is the place," Escobar said, pointing to a spot on the map.

Bolan studied the location. He traced it inland, then picked out Dupre's estate. Using a rule, he estimated he was some twenty miles off.

Escobar watched him, his expression changing as he recognized the Dupre estate.

"It is not a good place," he said.

Bolan nodded. "I know, but it is important that I go there."

The man pointed to the Uzi that Bolan had placed on the chart table.

"To kill him?"

"I might have to."

"Then do it, and do it well. For all of us."

20

This time Bolan went in fully prepared. He knew his priorities and his targets.

The situation called for direct action. There was no time left for waiting. Dupre was moving ahead. The next move would be to ship out his illicit bomb on its final journey.

Bolan was satisfied in his own mind that Dupre was aiming his bomb at America itself. Where exactly, he had yet to determine.

The colonel had a major grievance against the U.S. It had been U.S. armed forces, on the direct order of the President, who had stepped in to oust Dupre, not only to put a stop to the atrocities he committed, but also to defuse a situation that had the potential to explode and drag in the rest of the Caribbean.

The ex-dictator had, from his safe haven, done everything he could to discredit America, accusing it of blatant misuse of power.

There was little anyone could do about Dupre's accusations, or his threats, as long as he stayed on

Cielo. Most of his rantings were dismissed as hot air. Now, though, that hot air seemed likely to be turned into a blast of something far more deadly. If—and the more Bolan thought about it, the more he became convinced he was right—Dupre was going to use his bomb for a revenge attack, then the U.S. would be at the top of his list. Dupre had long been branded unstable. His wild and brutal mood swings were infamous. His need to save face was also one of his known qualities, and he had killed more than once to extricate himself from embarrassing situations.

Now it was shaping up to the ultimate face saver, the ultimate act of revenge. The Colonel had spent more than two years and countless millions of dollars to bring about the creation of his nuclear weapon. He wasn't going to use it casually.

Escobar brought them to the Dupre estate. The Colombian's claim to know Cielo well proved to be no lie. The man had guided Bolan through miles of dense forest with ease.

It was midday when they reached the edge of the forest. They crouched behind a massive fallen tree trunk and assessed the situation below them.

The estate lay at the base of a slight slope, and from their elevated position, Bolan was able to identify the landscape. To his left lay the coastline, with the beach below where he had taken on Dupre's bodyguards. He traced a line back, around the tennis courts and the swimming pool, to the blackened shell of the garages.

"They had a fire," Escobar remarked. "Were you here, then?"

"I might have had a hand in it."

Escobar chuckled. "I can believe that."

Bolan saw a car parked at the front of the house. He watched as a familiar figure stepped from it to talk to a man who'd come out of the house.

The visitor was Captain Varro.

"I know that one!" Escobar said, making no attempt to conceal his hatred of the man. "He is a monster."

Bolan didn't answer. When Escobar glanced around, he saw that the American was checking his weaponry. There had been an arms cache on board the boat. Long-barreled 9 mm Uzis had been racked in a cupboard. Beneath them, in a lower section, were half a dozen SIG-Sauer P-226 9 mm pistols. The final prize had been a pair of Ithaca Model 37s, shotguns with pistol grips. Bolan had equipped himself with two of the handguns and one of the shotguns. He'd found a leather satchel with a strap, which he'd looped over one shoulder and across his chest. Into that went magazines for the handguns, his Uzi and cartridges for the Ithaca.

Escobar had watched these preparations with wide eyes.

"Are you starting a war?" he'd asked.

"No, just carrying on an old one."

Escobar had turned to the cupboard and had stroked the sleek lines of the remaining shotgun.

"If you want it, take it," Bolan had said.

The Colombian had taken the weapon. He'd loaded it, stuffing a couple of boxes of shells into the pouch at his waist.

"Now I am ready!" he'd announced.

BOLAN COMPLETED his weapons' check.

"Escobar, this is as far as you go," he said.

"I will help you."

"You already have. Now it's my turn. These are evil people. The men who work for Dupre are murderers of woman and children. They torture for enjoyment. I can't let you become involved."

"Then I will wait here for you," Escobar replied. "I promise I will not follow you."

Bolan could see the stubborn gleam in the man's eyes.

"Okay," he conceded. "But don't come down there, whatever happens."

As Bolan turned to move out, he heard Escobar's whispered farewell.

"Go with God."

The Executioner wormed his way down the slight incline to reach the rear fence of the estate. As Escobar had promised, there was a blind spot where the forest had crept up to the perimeter fence, a mass of greenery that pushed hard against the steel mesh. Bolan eased his way deep into the foliage and found the place where the base of the fence had been pushed out by the undergrowth. By dropping on his back and putting his weapons through first, he was able to wriggle his way under the mesh and inside the perimeter fence. He gathered his weapons. Resettling the ammo bag, he slung the Uzi by its strap and brought the shotgun into play.

He worked his way to the edge of the foliage, crouching in the greenery while he checked out the house. There didn't seem to be a great deal of movement around the house, nor were there that many guards on duty, perhaps because he'd reduced Dupre's security force to a surviving few following the previous night's firefight. Bolan didn't spend too much time on speculating.

Scanning the rear of the house, he spotted a door. He made another area check, detected no movement and took off across the manicured lawn.

He gained the wall and flattened against it, checking the area. He edged along to the door and saw that it stood slightly open. He peered in through the gap, into the kitchen. It was a large, airy room that was fully equipped with all the latest in kitchenware. A large coffeepot sat simmering on a stove.

Suddenly Bolan heard a voice, the sound of someone approaching the kitchen. He sprinted to the door that led to the house, pressing himself against the wall.

The man who entered the kitchen had an Uzi slung over his shoulder. He was carrying a number of coffee mugs in both hands, which he dropped with a crash when he turned his head, spotting Bolan. He gave a warning yell as he reached for his weapon.

Bolan swung the stock of the shotgun, slamming it against the hardman's head. The man fell against the wall, clawing at it for support. The soldier jammed the butt into the bodyguard's lower back, drawing a low moan from him, then followed up with another blow to the back of his skull. The man went down with a hard thump. The Executioner relieved him of his Uzi, slinging it over his own shoulder.

As he turned back toward the door, he caught sight of a shadow falling across the floor. He stepped back, swinging the shotgun into position. As the figure lunged through the entrance, Uzi already tracking ahead of him, Bolan triggered the shotgun. The blast caught the Black Skull chest high, driving him back through the doorway.

Bolan exited the house, moving swiftly along the exterior wall until he reached the far corner. Edging around it, he scanned the immediate area and spotted a window. He turned his shotgun on it and triggered a shot that took out the glass and most of the frame. He vaulted over the windowsill to land in the room, dropping to a crouch behind a high-backed chair. He took a swift look around the room as he thumbed replacement cartridges into the shotgun, located the door and headed directly for it. As he eased it open, he caught a glimpse of two armed men hurrying down a tiled hallway.

There was a split second as the two parties sized up the situation.

Bolan raised the Ithaca and took out the lead man with a single blast, sending him into a stumbling, bloody fall. The hardman slithered across the floor, coming to a stop against the far wall.

The second man turned his Uzi on Bolan. The weapon unleashed a stream of 9 mm rounds at the wall and doorframe. Bolan ducked back inside the room, then heard the firing cease. He dropped to a crouch, pushed the shotgun ahead of him and triggered twice, sweeping the hall with a deadly hail of shot. The hardman caught enough to knock him off his feet. He crashed to the floor, cursing loudly, still dangerous as he hauled the Uzi around and began firing from his prone position.

Bolan heard the burst, felt the bullets cleave the air above his head. He dropped forward, stretching out on the floor, and fired the shotgun's final cartridges. The blast took the hardman full in the face, almost decapitating him.

Exchanging the shotgun for one of the Uzis, Bolan scrambled to his feet and headed along the hall. He emerged in the wide entrance hall of the house, the muzzle of the Uzi sweeping back and forth, searching for the room where Colonel Dupre had taken him to meet Dr. Semple.

Movement caught his eye, then he heard the unmistakable click of a weapon being cocked. The hardman who had emerged from a side door lost vital seconds readying his weapon before he could fire. Bolan didn't need to do that. He leveled his weapon and triggered a short burst. The hardman grunted as he felt the impact of the slugs burning into his chest. He slumped back against the wall, feebly pawing at the pain engulfing his body.

Bolan recognized the hallway that led to the secure room where Semple had been working. He headed in that direction, senses primed for any further sign of the Black Skulls inside the house.

He reached the end of the corridor. The door stood partway open. He wedged his foot against it and shoved.

The heavy door swung open, revealing an empty room. A scattering of papers lay on the work top where Bolan had seen the bomb casing. At the rear of the room, he located the deep safe that had most probably held the uranium 235. A thick metal door fitted with a combination lock stood open. The lead-lined interior was empty.

The next question Bolan needed answering concerned Dupre and Semple. Were they still here, or had they accompanied the bomb? And where to?

Bolan swung away from the safe and strode across the room. He reloaded the shotgun, his face grim. He was aware of time slipping away with alarming speed. Every minute separating him from Dupre and the nuclear device brought disaster closer. Bolan had followed a thin trail halfway across the world, only to have it slip through his fingers at each step. Having finally tracked the bomb to Cielo and Dupre, he couldn't allow it to vanish again. This time it would be on its way to whatever destination Dupre had chosen.

He pushed in the final cartridge, working the action to load the shotgun.

Images crowded his mind: Tanya Danovitch, killed in action on a mountain in Russia; Bob Lang, murdered in cold blood through an act of betrayal; Sol Benares, missing in action and presumed dead.

Each in his or her own way had helped Bolan reach this point in his mission. They had paid the ultimate price for their dedication.

For that alone, the Executioner was determined to stop Dupre's mad scheme.

And if that meant tearing the heart out of the ex-dictator's stronghold, then that was how it would have to be.

21

Three armed Black Skulls were in front of Bolan as he emerged from the hallway. They were on the point of splitting apart, one already turning to face the other way as the Executioner came into view.

The lead guard's shouted warning was lost in the blast from Bolan's shotgun. The charge flung the hardman backward, his own weapon clattering to the floor.

The remaining pair faced the warrior, weapons coming up simultaneously, one managing a short burst before Bolan's salvo from the shotgun cut them both down in a hail of blistering shot.

Bolan tossed the shotgun aside and pulled one of the Uzis into position. He prowled the hall, alert for further targets.

The house had fallen deathly quiet. He paused, ears tuned for any sound. Then he heard a faint noise from behind a closed door off to his left.

He crept to one side of the door, and eased it open, letting it swing wide.

From where he stood, he could see into a large, furnished room. Eight feet in, steps led down to a sunken main area. To the right of the door was a curving, highly polished bar counter. Behind it, a mirrored wall lined with shelves held bottles and glasses.

Bolan caught a flicker of movement in the mirror. Standing just to the left of the entrance, and clearly reflected in the glass, was Captain Varro, holding a handgun.

"Put the gun down, Varro, and step out."

The captain swung his head from side to side, trying to pinpoint the source of the voice.

"No second chance, Varro. Get rid of the gun, or you're dead like the rest of them."

Varro tossed his weapon aside, and raised his hands. Bolan moved swiftly through the door, his Uzi covering the man. The Executioner scanned the large room, noting that there were no other entrances. He pushed the door shut with his foot.

"Bad move," he said, "coming here and tying yourself in with Dupre."

"I am here on official business," Varro said.

"No," Bolan replied, "your business is cartel business, overseeing Dupre for your bosses on the mainland."

"Then you must realize what you've gotten yourself into. You will never leave Cielo alive," the man said.

Bolan's smile was thin and ice cold. "I think you have that the wrong way around."

He let his words sink in for a few seconds, saw the panic in Varro's eyes.

"You wouldn't dare kill me."

"Why not? All I see is a cheap little runner for the cartel, a piece of street scum playing cop."

Varro's anger, mingled with desperation, forced his next move. Despite the gun pointed at him, he launched a wild swing at the Executioner. The blow missed Bolan's jaw, pulling the captain around in a half circle. Bolan dropped to a crouch, under the punch, then swept the Uzi around as he straightened, catching Varro behind the ear. The blow pushed the man over the edge of the steps, and he tumbled to the floor. He lay there stunned, offering no resistance when Bolan grabbed hold of his shirt and hauled him to his feet. The soldier dragged him back up the steps and slammed him hard against the bar counter. He jammed the muzzle of the Uzi into the soft flesh beneath his captive's jaw.

"It's time to make decisions, Varro, like staying alive, or dying right here and now."

Images flashed through Varro's mind, of Dupre's bodyguards, lying scattered about the house, dead at the hand of the grim-faced man who now held his existence by a slender thread.

The police captain had always been in control, usually over those who were unable to resist. He had never faced such an opponent, and he found that his courage was less than he'd imagined it to be.

"What if I don't cooperate?"

Bolan's answer was to add an extra pound of pressure to the muzzle of the Uzi.

"Okay," the man gasped. "You want Dupre? And the doctor?"

The Uzi's pressure eased a fraction. Varro swallowed, sweat trickling down his face.

"They have gone to Pinto Bay, at the northeast end of the island."

"What's there?"

"A natural deep-water harbor. There used to be a coffee-refining plant there. When it went out of business the harbor was abandoned. Dupre has been using it to send and receive merchandise."

Bolan didn't need to ask what kind of merchandise Varro was talking about. The cargo Dupre was about to ship made narcotics seem harmless by comparison.

"When did they leave?"

"About two hours ago."

Bolan grabbed Varro's arm and pushed him to the door. With the Uzi covering the man, the Executioner walked him outside. Varro's car, with its police markings and equipment, caught the soldier's eye. If the vehicle was seen approaching the harbor, it would be assumed friendly. Any advantage was worth exploiting.

"Facedown on the ground."

Varro did as he was told.

Bolan checked out the car's interior. There was a shotgun secured in a rack to the right of the steering wheel. He removed it and placed it on the rear seat. He flipped open the glove box. Inside he found a clutter of equipment, including a stubby .38-caliber revolver and a pair of steel handcuffs. The keys for the cuffs went into Bolan's pocket, the revolver onto the rear seat.

Getting Varro back on his feet, Bolan ordered him into the driver's seat and cuffed his right wrist to the wheel. The soldier slid into the passenger seat.

"Let's go."

Varro tugged at the steel chain, anger blanketing his face.

"We wouldn't want you falling out," Bolan said. "Now drive."

Varro started the car and drove out through the open gates onto the narrow road.

"Step on it," Bolan said. "No one's going to give you a ticket."

The powerful car surged forward.

"How long will it take us?"

Varro shrugged, then answered quickly as Bolan raised the Uzi.

"About forty-five minutes."

"Try for less than that," Bolan suggested.

THEY MADE THE JOURNEY in just over thirty-five minutes. As the patrol car reached the summit of the hill overlooking the bay, Bolan had Varro pull over to the side of the road. When the vehicle came to a stop, the soldier reached across and took out the ignition key, dropping it into his shirt pocket.

"In case there're any accidents," he said as he climbed out, ignoring Varro's murderous scowl.

Bolan checked out the terrain. This end of the island was virtually uninhabited. All he could see were tracts of forest and lush vegetation. The road they were on was the only way in or out of the bay.

Pinto Bay itself was a wide, horseshoe-shaped expanse of calm blue water. It was half a mile across at its widest point, narrowing to three hundred yards at the end. The abandoned coffee refinery faced the exit to the sea. Administration buildings and warehouses lined one edge of the curving land area, separate from the refinery. A stone-and-concrete loading dock jutted into the water. Rusting machinery lay scattered about, and a traveling crane stood at the extreme tip of the dock.

There were a number of cars parked along the dock, as well as a large truck.

Moored at the dock was a nondescript cargo ship, the type generally referred to as a tramp steamer, the maritime equivalent of the pack mule. They plied their trade across the waterways, picking up cargo at different ports and delivering it where required.

Bolan saw that the steamer's funnel was emitting a thin spiral of black smoke. The diesel engines were still only turning over, which meant it wasn't yet ready to leave.

He returned to the patrol car and reinserted the ignition key.

"Time to drop in on your buddies," he said to Varro.

"This will never work," the captain said.

"They're your friends, Varro, don't you trust them?"

"Trust is for fools."

"You'll soon have an opportunity to find out. Now let's move."

A WIDE ROAD ran from the main highway to the bay area, with a striped drop bar closing off the entrance. At the side stood a wooden hut, occupied by a single, armed man. He stepped out of the structure as the patrol approached, his Uzi slung over one shoulder. When he recognized the police captain, he raised his hand in salute.

"Easy," Bolan said, pressing the muzzle of his weapon into Varro's side. "Let him come to us."

The guard peered at Bolan through the tinted windshield. Reaching the driver's-side window, he leaned in to speak and found himself staring down the muzzle of Bolan's Uzi.

"Hand me your gun," the soldier demanded. "Now!"

The hardman had no desire to catch a faceful of 9 mm slugs. He pulled his weapon from his shoulder and handed it over.

"Get to the front of the car," the Executioner said, "and lie across the hood."

He tracked the man's progress with the Uzi. Once the hardman was in position, Bolan took the keys from the ignition and stepped out of the car. Frisking the prone man, he relieved him of a Beretta 92-F and a black-handled switchblade. He removed the man's trouser belt and tied his hands behind his back, pulling the leather strap tight. He steered the hardman to the hut. There was a telephone fixed to the wall. Bolan cut the cable and used it to bind the man's ankles together.

"Do yourself a favor and stay here," the soldier said. "Show your face and I'll kill you."

He raised the drop bar before returning to the patrol car. He slipped the key back into the ignition and ordered Varro to drive on. The road ran in a wide curve, following the contours of the land before it straightened out to end at the cluster of buildings edging the bay.

Varro cruised along the road, sweat pouring down his face.

"We will both die. You are mad, American."

Varro knew Dupre's uncontrollable mood swings, the violent acts he was capable of. The Colonel had paid the captain handsomely to look out for his interests while he was resident on Cielo. That was on top of the money Varro received from the cartel. His instructions from them had been explicit: protect Dupre at all costs.

Varro had never trusted Dupre, but he was caught in a no-win situation. If he disobeyed the cartel, he was a dead man. If he went against Dupre, he was a dead man.

He had no options left open to him. He had to toe the line, to satisfy both masters.

He took his anger out on the visitors to the island, using his power as chief of police to fleece them at every turn. It wasn't a lot to brag about, but it was all he had.

Now this American had come, defying every authority on the island and storming Dupre's estate like some hero out of a TV show. Varro had to give the man his due. He knew his craft. The dead men littering the Dupre estate were evidence of that.

Whatever Mike Belasko was up to, the captain had a feeling he would succeed. The package Dupre and his American specialist had been assembling seemed to be at the heart of it. Varro had no idea what it was, nor did he care. All he wanted was to be rid of the whole damned mess.

"Hey, Varro! Ease up on the gas. Do you want to drop us both in the harbor?"

Bolan's voice interrupted Varro's musings. He switched his attention back to the approaching harbor complex.

It didn't matter about the outcome, he realized. Whether Belasko succeeded or not, he, Varro, was finished. He would be the scapegoat for either the cartel or Dupre, both of whom treated mistakes the same way.

They were paid for by the person who allowed them to happen.

It was said that the cartel had two ways of settling with offenders. If they were in a generous frame of mind, they killed you. If they weren't, they still killed you, but they did it with malice.

Either way you were dead.

Suddenly he jammed his foot hard on the gas pedal and sent the powerful car surging forward.

"Varro!" Bolan yelled.

The man ignored him. His face was gleaming with sweat, eyes staring straight ahead. The knuckles of his hands gleamed white where he gripped the wheel.

Bolan saw the harbor complex coming up fast and realized Varro had no intention of stopping.

He didn't have time to question the man's motives, or his state of mind. There was a single option, and Bolan took it.

He opened the car door and, tucking in his head, pushed himself away from the vehicle.

He hit the road with a stunning thump, the impact throwing him over and over. He came to a stop at the grass bank edging the road. He got to his feet and scrambled to the top of the bank, raising his head in time to see the careering patrol car slam headlong into one of the parked vehicles, shoving it along the concrete strip fronting the warehouses. Metal twisted and sheered. Sparks flew in orange tails. Then a ruptured fuel tank blew, and the area was engulfed in a ball of flame and smoke. A second blast tossed metal in every direction, sending Dupre's hardmen scattering.

With the confusion that followed, Bolan realized he would never get a better opportunity. He pushed to his feet and crept along the crest of the grass bank, then angled down to the rear of the administration building. A pall of smoke drifted across the area, pushed along by the breeze coming off the bay. It provided some cover, allowing Bolan to close in on the rear of the building. He crouched there, waiting for the smoke to drift his way. As the acrid cloud spilled along the side of the structure, he merged with it, hidden from view as he made for the front of the building.

Pressed against the wall, he watched the men on the dock haul thick ropes off the iron mooring posts. Midway along the cargo ship's hull, the gangplank was being drawn up. Thick smoke poured from the stack, and white foam erupted from the stern as the powerful propellers began to turn. The ship was leaving dock.

Yet again, Bolan was witnessing the nuclear bomb moving beyond his reach.

22

The scattered hardmen threw up a wall of resistance that Mack Bolan cut through with a blitzing force that had become his trademark.

The weapons he carried burned hot in his hands as he traded shots with the remnants of Colonel Dupre's bodyguards.

Used to dealing with terrified civilians who were easy to bully into submission, the Black Skulls had lost their edge during the months of idle living on the island estate. Faced with the Executioner's relentless onslaught, the guards offered something less than their best.

As he broke away from the administration building, Bolan encountered his first targets. A pair of armed hardmen, still dazed from the explosions that had turned their day into a living hell, found themselves face-to-face with the man who had already radically reduced their numbers.

Bolan's Uzi rattled sharply, penetrating the hardmens' bodies with 9 mm bullets. They were driven to the ground without even firing a shot.

Still making use of the swirling smoke from the car wrecks, the soldier cut to the right, coming up behind another pair of the colonel's henchmen. He cut down the gunners, puncturing their flesh with a long burst, emptying his magazine. Still moving, Bolan reversed the taped, double magazine and cocked the weapon.

He ducked behind a rusting heap of metal barrels, hearing the sharp ping of slugs striking the steel. Edging to the far side of the pile, at the very edge of the dock, Bolan leaned out and spotted the man responsible for the shooting. The hardman was shouting orders to someone outside Bolan's view. The Executioner silenced him with a short burst that took off the top of the man's head and dumped him facedown on the concrete.

The dead man's partner rushed forward in response to his cohort's shout, then saw he was too late. His head snapped around, eyes wide with alarm as he stood out in the open, with no cover close by.

The hardman spotted Bolan and opened up with his Heckler & Koch MP-5 subgun, the full-auto blast hammering a volley of slugs into the barrels only inches from where Bolan had been a moment before.

The Executioner had gone to ground, rolling away from the stacked drums. He came to rest on his stomach, the Uzi already up and tracking. He locked on to his target and stroked the trigger, blowing the hardman off his feet.

Sensing a threat close by, Bolan rolled, hearing the sharp burst of autofire. A stream of slugs chewed at the concrete, showering him with fragments. He pulled his upper body around, dropping the Uzi's muzzle, and triggered a long, hard blast that tore ragged holes in his target. The stricken man had time for a single, strangled yell before his body was slammed to the concrete and he bled out his last moments.

The steamer began to ease away from the dock, heading toward the blue waters of the bay. Bolan was only too aware of the vessel's progress. If he didn't get to it soon, it would clear the far end of the long dock, moving out into deeper water. Once it moved out to sea, he would lose it all together.

Crouching amid the havoc he'd brought down on Dupre's henchmen, Bolan scanned the dock site.

Some yards ahead stood the large truck that had undoubtedly transported the bomb. To one side of it was a powerful 4x4. It sported heavy tires and looked as if it could take on almost anything. Bolan wondered if it could face up to the cargo ship. He rose to his feet, eyes and ears open for any sign of Dupre's people. There didn't appear to be any more of them around.

He closed in on the 4x4. A chrome plate on the rear door told him what he needed to know—the all-terrain vehicle was fitted with a supercharged engine.

He opened the driver's door and leaned in. The keys were in the ignition. He dropped his Uzi on the leather seat, climbed in and fired up the engine.

He knew that he was taking a risk, but he had no other option. Once the cargo ship cleared the harbor it would be out of his hands.

The Executioner dropped the 4x4 into gear and slammed his foot on the gas pedal. The vehicle surged forward, tires burning and squealing, picking up speed at a tremendous rate. Bolan held it in the center of the dock as he closed the gap between himself and the cargo ship.

As he drew level with the stern, he could see men at the rail. They were pointing at the speeding 4x4. Automatic weapons were produced, muzzle-flashes telling Bolan he was being fired on. Slugs hammered at the vehicle's body, struck the windshield. None did any damage. A wry smile curled Bolan's mouth. Dupre's 4x4 had been built from bullet-proof steel, the windows made up of armored glass.

He moved up to a higher gear, feeling the engine smooth out. The end of the dock was still a fair distance away, but he was approaching it at an increasing pace. He was going to have to make his move soon.

He checked out the ship. The gap between it and the dockside was no more than three to four feet, but that would increase quickly as the propellers built up their thrust.

Bolan was running alongside the steamer now. Its deck was only inches below the level of the dock. Apart from hatch covers and securing clamps, the deck was clear of cargo containers.

As bullets continued to ricochet off the 4x4's body, Bolan caught sight of people leaning over the rail of the steamer's bridge gesturing wildly.

It was Colonel Dupre, with Dr. Semple at his side. Had they stayed on board deliberately, to oversee the bomb's safe dispatch, intending to leave the ship once everything was secured? Or had Bolan's unexpected arrival forced the pair into an unplanned trip?

He didn't care. If they got in his way, he would deal with them once he had the situation under control.

The dock end was too close for comfort. Bolan knew he had to make his play within the next few seconds.

He slammed the accelerator to the floor. The rising whine of the engine filled his ears. He eased the wheel slightly, swinging away from the water's edge to give himself a few extra feet, then swung the 4x4 back toward the edge of the dock.

The hurtling vehicle cleared the edge, the engine screaming as the wheels lost traction. For what seemed an eternity the 4x4 hung in the air, then began to drop.

Still moving forward, its wheels spinning, the hurtling vehicle crashed onto the deck of the cargo ship. It bounced and rocked its way along, tires howling and leaving streaks of rubber behind.

Bolan hung on to the wheel, as he was slammed back and forth. One of the side windows shattered as the 4x4's bodywork was twisted out of alignment by the battering. A crack zigzagged across the windshield.

Jamming his foot on the brake, Bolan tried to bring the speeding vehicle under control, but it went into a slithering skid. One of the tires burst as it was slammed against a metal projection and the 4x4 slewed in a half circle, coming to rest against the aft bulkhead with a wrenching impact. A burst of steam erupted from beneath the crumpled hood, and oil spewed from the sump. Bolan smelled burning wiring, and smoke began to creep from beneath the dashboard.

He snatched up his Uzi and booted open the passenger door. He rolled out of the 4x4, dropping to a crouch in the gap between the vehicle and the bulkhead that had halted its slide.

A door in the bulkhead swung open feet away from Bolan, an armed man framed in the opening. The soldier dived, slamming his shoulder to the door, driving it shut. The thick metal caught the gunman's head, crushing it against the frame, and he slumped to the deck. Bolan slipped through the hatch, hearing the clang of bullets striking the steel plate behind him.

He was in a narrow companionway. Metal steps led to the bridge section. Bolan went up fast, ducking as he reached the top. A volley of autofire ricocheted off the metalwork. He returned fire, catching his assailant in the upper legs.

Bolan crouched low, catfooting along the side of the bridge, aware that he was still vulnerable to attack from any number of positions. He slipped in behind a web of metal posts as the thump of running feet reached him. He waited until the gunners came into view before kicking them off their feet with a sustained burst from the Uzi.

The subgun locked on an empty breech. Bolan ejected the spent magazine and reached into his bag for a fresh one. He clicked it home, cocked the weapon and broke cover to move along the companionway. As he skirted the front of the main bridge, he saw startled faces behind the glass of the wheelhouse. A beefy man in a peaked cap began to yell, pointing Bolan out to an armed hardman from Dupre's team. The gunner responded by firing at the Executioner through the glass. With shards falling around him, Bolan scooted to the opposite side, then returned fire. His volley caught the hardman as he peered through the shattered glass, searching for his target. He twisted, his own finger jerking back against the trigger, spraying the wheelhouse with a lethal burst of fire. Caught in the random blast, the man in the peaked cap and the helmsman went down.

A shadow fell across Bolan. He ducked and heard the clang of metal against metal. A man cursed, grunting with effort as he swung his implement. This time it connected, a solid blow that caught Bolan's right arm, knocking the Uzi from his grasp. The weapon skidded across the deck out of reach.

Turning to face his adversary, Bolan looked upon Colonel Dupre's rage-darkened features. The man was taking another swing at Bolan with the heavy fire extinguisher he'd snatched from a holder on the bulkhead. This time Bolan ducked under the awkward swing. He slammed both fists between Dupre's legs, the blow drawing a scream of agony from the man. With a grimace of pain drawing back his lips, Dupre attempted to throw the extinguisher at Bolan. The Executioner raised his arms to ward off the impact, then realized that Dupre had lost his balance and was following the path of the extinguisher. He tried to avoid the man's headlong rush, but it was too late. They crashed to the deck, locked together in a deadly embrace.

Bolan slammed an elbow to the side of Dupre's temple, stunning him. Levering himself into a sitting position, he grabbed Dupre's head with both hands, and slammed his face into the steel plate of the bulkhead. Shoving the unconscious man aside, the Executioner lurched to his feet.

"If he can't stop you, I will!"

Bolan turned to see Ralph Semple standing ten feet away. He held a SIG-Sauer P-226 pistol, his hand visibly shaking.

"You don't have the guts," Bolan said. "You can only kill at a distance, pressing a button to set off a bomb that will kill thousands. Just as long as you don't have to see the results up close."

"Don't bet on it," Semple said. "After what you've done, I want nothing more than to kill you."

Bolan kept his eyes locked on Semple, even as he dropped to one knee, his right hand reaching for his own P-226 tucked behind his belt, even up to the moment he leveled the pistol and put three bullets into Semple while the other man was still thinking about it. The physicist went down without a sound, blood pulsing from the dark holes in his shirt, directly over his heart.

"If you're going to do it, then do it. Don't talk about it," Bolan said quietly.

He heard a rustle of sound and saw Dupre dragging himself to his feet, hanging on to the metal rail edging the companionway.

Blood coursed down the colonel's face, dripping from his chin onto his shirt that was streaked with dirt. He stared at Bolan, defiance showing in his cold eyes.

"I will not stand trial," he said. "Do not underestimate my influence, Belasko. If the law can't be persuaded to free me, then it will have to be bought."

"I had a feeling you might say that," Bolan replied. "I can't allow that to happen."

Dupre cackled and made a move toward a hideaway pistol, holstered at the small of his back.

A trio of shots to the head stopped Dupre in his tracks and ended his plan for revenge.

Bolan scooped up the Uzi and went to the bridge rail overlooking the cargo deck. Smoke was still coming from the wrecked 4x4.

A number of armed men were edging toward the companionway that would give them access to the bridge. Bolan strafed them with a long burst from the Uzi, sending the armed men scattering.

"Dupre is dead. It's over" he yelled. "Take your chances. Get off this ship now. If you don't, I'll kill any man I find."

He raked the deck area again, emptying the magazine. While the crew remained under cover, Bolan reloaded.

"I can do it," he said. "Your captain is dead, so is the helmsman. Dupre isn't going to be around to pay you off, either. This vessel is sailing itself right now, so make your choice before we reach open water."

The ship's slow progress across the harbor allowed the crew to make the sensible choice. Men below decks were called up to join the others. They stood around, discussing the situation for a few minutes, then Bolan watched them toss a pair of inflatable life rafts into the water and board them. They began to paddle back toward the dock, leaving Bolan alone on the steamer.

He took the wheel and guided the craft through the harbor entrance and out to sea. Once clear, he steered away from the island. He held a straight course, watching for any sign he was being tracked. He saw and heard nothing. If Dupre had had a standby craft waiting, it didn't show.

Only when he'd cleared Colombian waters, did he allow himself to relax. He turned on the radio, keying in a setting he'd been given before leaving Stony

Man Farm, and opened a transmission. He received a reply almost immediately.

"We have a fix on you, Striker. Stand by. ETA is forty minutes."

Bolan went out on deck and leaned against the rail. He felt tired but satisfied. The U.S. Navy submarine that had been waiting for his signal would show soon, and the experts would take over, locating and disarming the nuclear device on the ship. Once that was done, his mission was over. There would be the usual debriefing once he returned to the Farm. He didn't anticipate a great deal of protesting or repercussions: The principal players in the game were dead, and those on the fringes would be too busy covering their own tracks to make a fuss.

As far as Bolan was concerned, the important consideration was the removal of the threat to the United States. This time they had stopped it.

This time.

EPILOGUE

War Room, Stony Man Farm

Mack Bolan finished reading the file and laid it on the table. The documents had been recovered from Ralph Semple's briefcase, along with other data relating to the planned detonation of the uranium bomb. He raised his eyes and looked at Hal Brognola.

"They had it worked out well. Exploding that bomb in the middle of the Kansas corn belt was clever thinking. The radiation would have rendered the land unfit for years."

"Dupre meant his revenge to have a lasting effect," Brognola said. "The guy was crazy, but he knew what he wanted. Look at the planning that went into the compartment in the keel of the cargo ship. It took the Navy boys over eight hours to locate it. That thing was so well hidden it would've gotten by normal inspection. Sealed, radiation-proof. Scary stuff when you think it was all down to one man on a revenge trip.''

''This one came too close to happening,'' Bolan said. ''The problem is, how do we prevent a repeat? Look how easy it was for them to get their uranium, someone to process it, have a bomb casing made, then almost bring it all together.''

Brognola sighed as he unwrapped a cigar.

''Don't remind me, Mack, I've been burning ears all down the line over this. The Russians are falling over themselves to convince us they won't let thefts occur again. I believe they mean it. Next time around the bomb might be aimed at them. Hell, they even thanked us for the information on Sheppard's gun-running outfit. Apparently they busted the operation wide open.''

The mention of Russia reminded Bolan of Tanya Danovitch, which led him to thoughts of Bob Lang and Sol Benares—all good people, dead because they cared enough to put themselves in the line of fire.

And here he was, still alive. Battered and bruised maybe, but still alive.

The only reason he could see why was to insure the deaths of those good people hadn't been in vain. He was the one left to carry on the fight, to wage War Everlasting.

If the enemy had considered him tough opposition previously, they were in for a bigger shock next time around. That was a promise Mack Bolan made to his fallen comrades, and the Executioner always made good on his promises.

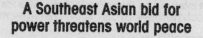

Don't miss out on the action in these titles featuring
THE EXECUTIONER®, STONY MAN™ and SUPERBOLAN®!

The Red Dragon Trilogy

#64210	FIRE LASH	$3.75 U.S.	☐
		$4.25 CAN.	☐
#64211	STEEL CLAWS	$3.75 U.S.	☐
		$4.25 CAN.	☐
#64212	RIDE THE BEAST	$3.75 U.S.	☐
		$4.25 CAN.	☐

Stony Man™

#61907	THE PERISHING GAME	$5.50 U.S.	☐
		$6.50 CAN.	☐
#61908	BIRD OF PREY	$5.50 U.S.	☐
		$6.50 CAN.	☐
#61909	SKYLANCE	$5.50 U.S.	☐
		$6.50 CAN.	☐

SuperBolan®

#61448	DEAD CENTER	$5.50 U.S.	☐
		$6.50 CAN.	☐
#61449	TOOTH AND CLAW	$5.50 U.S.	☐
		$6.50 CAN.	☐
#61450	RED HEAT	$5.50 U.S.	☐
		$6.50 CAN.	☐

(limited quantities available on certain titles)

TOTAL AMOUNT	$
POSTAGE & HANDLING	$
($1.00 for one book, 50¢ for each additional)	
APPLICABLE TAXES*	$_____
TOTAL PAYABLE	$_____
(check or money order—please do not send cash)	

To order, complete this form and send it, along with a check or money order fo the total above, payable to Gold Eagle Books, to: **In the U.S.:** 3010 Walden Avenu P.O. Box 9077, Buffalo, NY 14269-9077; **In Canada:** P.O. Box 636, Fort Erie, Ontari L2A 5X3.

Name:_____

Address:_____ City:_____

State/Prov.:_____ Zip/Postal Code:_____

*New York residents remit applicable sales taxes.
  Canadian residents remit applicable GST and provincial taxes.

GEBACK1

When all is lost, there is always the future

JAMES AXLER

DEATH LANDS ®

Skydark

It's now generations after the firestorm that nearly consumed the earth, and fear spreads like wildfire when an army of mutants goes on the rampage. Ryan Cawdor must unite the baronies to defeat a charismatic and powerful mutant lord, or all will perish.

In the Deathlands, the future is just beginning.

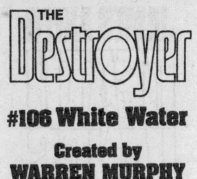